CALENDAR OF GHOSTS
A novel in twelve months

JASON COBLEY

Eutierria Publishing

DEDICATION

To everyone who has ever lost someone you loved.

Also by Jason Cobley

A Hundred Years to Arras

The Mines of Arras and Other Stories

Taking Liberties - A Short Story Anthology (contributor

THE GHOST OF CHRISTMAS NEVER

T his winter, this season of freezing and forgiveness, embraced everyone with its bitterness. It banished memories of fingers intertwined with sunlight, in the meadow, under the trees. December enveloped the night with longing, with remembrances of childhood lost in the winter fog.

Christmas was not always like this. Before World War Two, there was warmth, and family, and eiderdowns. There was jam and running in the woods. During the war, there was cold, and absence, and mending socks. There was fire and running to the shelter. Afterwards, there was making do and getting by. Make do with Mum and get by without Dad.

Derek's father was a bombardier who never came home one Christmas. The boy was eight years old and waited at the foot of the stairs for the rattle of keys and the front door to swing open. He stayed there all Christmas Day while his mother cried in the kitchen. Derek's father had died, it was reported, heroically, but his body was never found. Ironically, as the man tasked with loading bombs, it was a German bomb that got him, or so it seemed. Not so much as a button off his uniform was recovered.

That was 1943. On Christmas Eve 1944, Derek woke after midnight, lit a candle balanced in an empty teacup, and sat on the stairs, hoping that this Christmas might be the one when his father came home. He was waiting for that time when the door would open and Dad would lift him in his arms. His eyelids grew heavy and soon, without him noticing, he was asleep, his head against the bannister. In his dream, he was in his pyjamas and dressing gown, slippers sliding in the mud, as he stood on the edge of a battlefield. The mist drew in as his feet sank slowly into the wet earth. It became a muggy fog, opaque and thick like oatmeal. The sounds of clashing metal and rifles cracking the air called to him. The fog parted as a figure, dark and tall, moved towards him. Derek's eyes blurred with tears. He blinked, then his eyes fluttered open.

Awake, he felt the wooden stair hard and flat against him. He stared straight ahead. A vertical slice of light separated the front door from its frame as it slowly swung open towards him. Lit brightly from behind, almost in silhouette, a man now stood in the doorway. It was a man wearing a bombardier's uniform. The father smiled vacantly down at the son, who cried and flung out his arms in a desperate embrace. His hands met cold air and a closed door.

His mother stayed in the house even after the boy became the man, got married and left home, but every Christmas Eve, Derek would arrive in the morning and stay until she had gone to bed, when he would sit on the stairs and, for a few moments, be nine years old again.

Every year, he hoped that his father would once more open the door, drop his kitbag on the floor, and open his arms to his only child.

In time, Derek's mother died, and he moved into the house with his own family. His own son Owen was born in the winter of 1963 and, eventually, made Derek a grandfather. Kathryn Dark was born in 1995. She doted on her grandparents until they passed away and the house was inherited by Owen, her father. Kathryn was still a toddler when Mum and Dad took ownership of the house.

It was December 2018, and nobody was in when Kathryn knocked on the front door. Or, at least, there didn't seem to be to her. It was dark. No lights were on. Only a streetlight illuminated the driveway from the pavement. It was harsh, bright, white: one of the new LED streetlights. Much less atmospheric than the yellowy glow of older lamps, but the atmosphere was not what she was looking for. She was looking for her father.

Kathryn ruffled in her handbag again for keys, but vainly. She looked like she knew they weren't there. It had been so long since she was last there that she thinks she might have lost them down the back of a sofa or under Carl's bed. She was probably so drunk one night that she kicked her bag over and everything spilled over the bedroom floor. She would have bent down to pick things up but fallen over and then Carl tumbled on to the bed with her and that was that. Gathering her things together in the morning, it would be in haste, so she wouldn't miss the bus, so the keys could still be there. It's highly unlikely that Carl ever cleaned under the bed, so he wouldn't have noticed.

So anyway. Dad. Kathryn knocked again. No answer. It was icy cold. There was no chance of a white Christmas but a wet, cold, dull, and dreary one was on the cards. Christmas lights sparkled down the street, blinking blindly their devotion.

'Dad! It's me! I forgot my keys!' Kathryn called, banging with the side of her fist now. The door thudded, solid in its frame.

'Are you looking for Owen? Are you sure he's in?' The question came from over the fence, a low one on the drive shared with the neighbour. Diminutive in height but large in volume, Barbara was there in her dressing gown over admittedly quite stylish boots. Retired, grey in curls and white in teeth, Barbara peered down the side of the house, which was dark, unlit, and empty but for the bins.

'Oh, hello Barbara. Yes, I'm sure he's in. I rang him when I arrived at the station and again when I got in the Uber on my way over'. Kathryn resumed banging on the door.

'I don't think he can hear you. Don't you have a key?'

'I do, but I think I lost it. Dad!'

A light came on in the hall, visible through the frosted glass pane in the door. This house was born in a previous century, but the door was newer, hence the frosted glass. There was a shuffling and some muttering, growing louder as a blur neared the door.

'Who is it?' growled the voice from inside.

Kathryn sighed. Barbara shrugged, waved, and went back into her own dimly lit house. 'It's me, Dad. Kathryn. I just spoke to you twenty minutes ago from the taxi.'

'Oh. Alright. Come on in, then.'

'I haven't got my key. You need to open it from inside.'

'Oh, right. Hang on.' Some rattling and the sliding of a bolt, then the door was open. Warm air opened out like a hand as Kathryn stepped in. She stooped and hugged the old man. To be fair, he wasn't all that old, but he seemed to act older sometimes. He was in his fifties, having fathered Kathryn in his early thirties. Sometimes it seemed that his responsibility had stopped there.

'Didn't you hear me knocking?' she asked, putting her bags down in the hall.

'No. Well, I did. I was arguing with somebody.' Kathryn followed Dad through to the kitchen. 'There's somebody here?'

'No.' He filled the kettle, clicked it on. 'On the internet.'

'Oh, you've not been arguing with strangers about Brexit again, have you?'

He banged a pair of mugs down on the kitchen worktop. 'Two days before Christmas and parliament have gone on holiday with no deal sorted out. These Tory bastards in their ivory castles dripping with gold, lording over us minions, counting the cash their business interests are going to rake in when we crash out of the EU with no jobs, no future... ah bollocks, I've had enough.'

'Well, yeah. It's Christmas though. And I'm here,'

9

Kathryn said, trying to change the subject.

'Theresa Bloody May,' he muttered, as he dropped a teabag into each cup. 'Lying witch.'

'Can I have coffee, Dad?'

He picked out the teabag and popped it into his mug alongside the other one. 'I'll have a double then. Coffee it is for you, Miss Picky.'

'Thanks Dad.' She watched him pouring the steaming water, then took her mug, cradled it as a hand warmer. 'She's not a witch, though. I don't know of any coven who'd have her.'

'Well, you'd know.'

'Very funny. Yes. Yes, I would. Psychology is witchcraft. I get it. Ha ha.'

'You're not still on that, are you? Studying and all that? Did you ever get on a proper course at university?'

'Hilarious, Dad. Yes, and yes. Got any biscuits?' Kathryn started opening cupboards.

The centre of the kitchen was a hefty pine table, handmade years earlier. Kathryn sat, sipping her coffee, running her fingers over the smooth undulations of the table's surface. Here was where she'd drawn a star with biro when she was eight and had been forced to scrub the ink off. The shape was still carved into the wood, part of it now. Here was the burn mark where Dad had placed a hot pan whilst trying – and failing - to make jam. The whole strawberry-smelling boiling mess had gone in the bin. Here was where Mum had stabbed out her last cigarette.

A half-empty packet of custard creams landed on the table.

'These are a bit soft, Dad. How long have you had

these?'

'Oh, I don't know. Last year sometime. I don't really eat biscuits.'

He sat opposite her, wincing at his strong tea. 'So.'

'Yes, Dad?'

'It's lovely to see you, but... why now?'

'It's Christmas. Thought I'd come and stay with my Dad at Christmas.'

Tentatively, he put a hand on hers, half intending it to be a parental squeeze, but instead it becomes a pat, and a brief one at that. He withdrew, tucked his hand under the table. Kathryn looked at her hand, where her father's touch had briefly visited.

'I mean,' he said, 'it's been three years, Kitty.'

She laughed, almost a snort. Stifling it quickly, she said, 'Oh, sorry! It's just – no one's called me that in years. Kathryn always. Or Miss Dark. I've started getting that now. Guess I'm just getting old.'

'Not to me. You don't look any different, just a little...'

'What?'

'Suppose it's the big boots, the ripped jeans and the big jumper. And your hair.'

'My hair?' Involuntarily, she ran her fingers through her fringe.

'Well, it's a lot shorter. When did you get it cut?'

'Ages ago. I...' She avoided her father's gaze. 'I'm sorry it's been so long, Dad.'

'That's – well, it's good you're here now, for Christmas.'

No snow, although it was Christmas Eve. It wasn't Dickensian London. It was this town in 2018, all coffee, second-hand bookshops and hairdressers. Kathryn looked up and down the road. Not much had changed. There was an alleyway opposite the house where the high street could be glimpsed. Kathryn always used to talk about the bookshop at the top of the street, and complain about parking at Sainsbury's, which was way down the bottom. Dad stayed in much more now, since the second-hand record shop, situated above the barbers, had gone, decamped to another town in search of hipsters or middle-aged men willing to haggle over the price of old progressive rock albums.

'What you lookin' at?' The voice came from Mike, the old school friend she was waiting to meet outside this house.

'Oh, just reminiscing,' she said.

They hugged, the squeeze of old friends.

'Drink?' he said.

'Can't. Got to get back in for Dad in a minute.'

Sitting on the wall outside the house, they zipped their coats up more tightly, and said as one, 'So...' They both laughed. 'You go,' Kathryn said.

'Okay,' Mike sighed, combing his curly hair through his fingers. He smoothed under his chin with the back of his hand, perhaps trying to hide the extra weight he had put on since they last saw each other. 'It's brilliant to hear from you, but it's been ages. Gotta ask: why now? Merry Christmas, by the way.'

'Dad asked the same question.'

'Yeah?'

'I told him a different answer.'

'You haven't given me an answer yet.'

'Well,' she paused, setting down her drink. 'I heard from my Mum.'

Mike was puzzled. 'But your Mum's dead,' he said.

Kathryn ignored the kindly tone, used as if Mike was comforting her in a delusion. 'I know,' she laughed, and then, suddenly serious, she stared at the ground. 'For a long time after she died, I couldn't bear to come home. I kept in touch with Dad. That's what phones are for. And he came to visit me. But I couldn't come back to the house. Not for three years. Not until now.'

'But... I mean...'

'How?'

'Well, yeah.'

She raised her eyes to meet Mike's. As if the absurdity of what she was about to say only now dawned on her, she blushed. 'I... got this text,' she said.

He nodded, and thought for a moment, weighing up how to respond. 'You know anyone could send you a text, right? It doesn't mean...'

'It came from Mum's number.'

'Maybe someone got hold of her phone, maybe the number was reallocated, maybe there's a problem with your phone. Could be anything, Kath.'

'Yeah, I know.'

'If you don't mind me asking, what did it say? This text from beyond the grave?' He did spooky wavy fingers to lighten up the conversation.

'Well, that's just it. It didn't make much sense. I did

wonder whether Dad had done it. But he isn't being any more weird than normal, so I don't know what to think.'

Mike zipped up his coat and bumped down off the wall. 'Well, if you're not coming to the pub, I'll see you tomorrow.'

Kathryn joined him and gave him a quick hug. 'Tomorrow?'

'You didn't think I'd let Christmas Day go by without popping in, did you? I'll need to walk off my Mum's sprouts anyway, I expect.'

'Fair enough. No idea whether Dad's even got any food in. Might be a beans on toast Christmas for us. We'll see.'

Mike took a step away, then turned back, his eyes sparkling with curiosity. 'I've got to know, though. What did the text say?'

'Oh, nothing really. Like I said, it didn't make any sense. It just read "make do", and nothing else.'

Kathryn managed to find a takeaway that would deliver on Christmas Eve, so after duck chow mein and spring rolls, she sat with her father in the kitchen, cradling a glass of red wine. Frost had already started to form again outside, white and sparkling in the night against the window. The cold was holding the house in boneless, bloodless hands. Dad held forth on politics, how the country was going down the drain, and how there was worse to come. Kathryn agreed with some of it, indulged most of it. Politics wasn't her thing.

'Dad?' she said, sensing the right gap in the conversation.

'Yes?'

'Did you send me a text from Mum's old phone?'

He turned away, taking the used plates to the sink without scraping the leftovers into the bin. Noodles slid into the soapy water. 'No,' he said, with his back to Kathryn.

'Aren't you going to ask me why?'

He was scooping the food out of the water into a bowl. 'All right then. Why?'

'Dad? Can you look at me?'

When he faced his daughter again, there were tears in his eyes. The skin under each one suddenly seemed heavier.

'No. I did wonder whether you had received one.'

'What do you mean?'

'I have too.'

He sat facing his daughter, downed his wine, refilled the glass, then took a deep breath before continuing. He breathed out through his nose, as if cleansing himself. It seemed to calm him. 'Kitty,' he began at last, 'do you remember my father?'

'Grandad Derek? Of course I do. This used to be his house, him and Grandma.'

'And his parents before that. We've always kept it in the family. Did I ever tell you about when his father - my grandfather - died?'

'In the war, wasn't it?'

'Yes, that's what everyone thought. At Christmas. Every Christmas Eve into morning, Derek sat on the stairs in this house, waiting, hoping that one year would be the year that his father came home.'

'He never did, though, did he? At Christmas?'

'He was dead, no doubt about that. But one time, I did ask my father whether he did see him. Just to see what he'd say. I expected to get a flea in my ear for being cheeky.'

'What did he say?'

'Nothing. He wouldn't answer. He just made me promise that I wouldn't sell the house. I mean, your mother and I were only too glad to sell our little box and move in. Your mother...' His voice grew quiet and his attention wandered to the marks on the table. He ran his fingers along the smooth grain. 'Why did you leave it so long to come home?' he asked.

'Oh, Dad, we've been through this. When Mum got sick, it was hard for me. When she died, I had university... It just upset me too much. I just needed some time. But I'm here now. And it's not like we haven't seen each other at all, is it? And you're doing okay, aren't you?' she replied. Her hand hovered momentarily above his before giving it a comforting pat.

'Are you staying here tonight?'

'Of course, Dad. It's Christmas.'

'Okay. If you hear me banging about in the middle of the night, just ignore it and go back to sleep. I don't sleep very well. Old man problems. So sometimes I just get up for a cup of tea before I go back.'

Kathryn quickly realised that dancing around their family history like this was the closest she was going to get to any answers. Dad must have charged up Mum's old phone and sent an old text by accident, or equally accidentally pressed a button or two and predictive text did the rest. There were dozens of plausible explanations.

Back in her childhood bedroom, sleep came quickly. The cold wind rattled the old windows, a familiar sound that reassured her, reminding her of wintry nights as a little girl, cosy under her warm duvet. Kathryn wove in and out of sleep, restless, until a sound woke her. Heavy footsteps creaked across the landing and down the stairs. She knew them to be her father's and was comforted, until they stopped, seemingly halfway down the staircase. The sigh of a soft settling of weight suggested that her father had sat on the stairs. She held her breath and waited, listening for the slightest sound. Nothing. Maybe Dad had collapsed. Kathryn pulled back the duvet and padded towards her bedroom door. Just to check on him. Just as she reached for the door handle, a soft murmuring, a barely audible whisper, made her pause.

Her phone buzzed on the bedside table, the vibrations through the wood deep and throaty. She recoiled.

'What the... Jesus, that made me jump,' she said aloud, despite her best instincts.

The screen was lit, showing a notification. Kathryn held the shining rectangle in her hand. She opened the messaging app. The screen showed the sender of the text as 'Mum'. Kathryn felt her cheeks prickle and a draught chilled her neck. She read the text. 'Merry Christmas,' it said.

Outside the door, the whispering intensified:

indistinct but harsh; words blending but two voices. Two voices that she knew.

On the landing, with the bedroom door open behind her, Kathryn saw her father slumped against the bannister, sitting on a stair. The front door was a few feet away from the foot of the stairs. It was ajar, a bright white light from outside cutting through the shadows. The light framed one of the shadows in an ephemeral mist. The shape was shifting, moving, stepping up the stairs towards her father. The shape had hair that cascaded over its shoulders. The body continued with the curves of a mother and a skirt that merged with the darkness below. A face, lips and eyes just suggestions in the night, leaned in close to Kathryn's father. 'Owen,' she heard the voice say. The voice of her mother.

Kathryn felt her eyes close and a weakness overcome her. A knocking roused her. She came to her senses, kneeling on the carpet on the landing. It was daylight. The morning sun streamed through the front door as Mike stepped through. 'Kathryn! You okay?' he called. And then he paused, noticing her father, slumped against the bannister on the stairs.

Kathryn took a seat beside him, touched his face, then squeezed his wrist. Cold, peaceful and still, as if sleeping. He had waited on the stairs for his wife, and she came.

RADIO WAVES

T he snow thickened at the base of the wall that edged the car park. A hastening wind was causing it to drift in one direction, and it was quickly settling. Daryl Thomson had parked the car awkwardly across two spaces. His wheels had spun when he tried to manoeuvre the Fiesta into a straighter position, so he decided to leave it where it came to rest, less likely to roll if the handbrake failed and probably easier to reverse back out when the time came to leave. He only had fifteen minutes until his show was due to start anyway, so time was not on his side.

Laden with a shoulder bag containing a selection of records, compact discs and notebooks, Daryl negotiated the icy incline up to the door of the community centre. He tapped in the door code, took the keys for the studio out of the wall safe, and made his way through the function room, the so-called "youth room", to the studio door.

The radio studio was little more than a cupboard, really. A mixing desk hooked up to two personal computers occupied one corner of the room. An antiquated industrial-sized CD player and broken record deck combo was balanced on an adjacent table, a mess of cabling meeting the computers somewhere in the dusty darkness behind them. One screen ran the radio broadcasting software; the other hosted digital files of a fair array of music. Daryl used to come armed with a stack of crackling records, but since the belt broke on the turntable, he increasingly had to rely on uploading mp3 files from a memory stick. Over the previous few months, he had gradually populated the folders with enough of his favourite music to be able to program several shows, so he was content, even if his rare John Coltrane live performances and deleted punk singles had to stay at home. He was king of his own domain for a couple of hours each week. His own radio show.

The opposite corner of the room was a mess of abandoned old equipment, boxes overflowing with cables, too-small t-shirts screen printed with the station logo, and plastic bags stuffed with random rubbish that had just been dumped there. No one else took responsibility for tidying it, so he wasn't going to. Everyone who presented a show on the radio station was a volunteer. That included Daryl. He settled into the chair, straightened the rickety arm as best he could, and began setting up. He laid out his notebook and pen, plugged in his headphones, adjusted the microphone, with its spit shield, to the correct height, and took a sip from his bottle of water.

With a sigh, he scooped up the empty sandwich wrapper left by the previous presenter. He threw it at the bin, but it bounced off the overflowing contents into the corner of the room, where a pile of donated Daniel O' Donnell CDs lay, forgotten and unplayed. Most things in the room were donated or paid for from the funds allocated by the community centre's trustees. They had been in place since austerity cuts had nearly forced its closure several years ago. It was unique for the town to have its own internet radio station alongside the rooms used for Weight Watchers, dance classes and youth clubs, but it was only able to operate at all by volunteers giving their time to present shows.

Most of the time, the music had to be automated, and it cycled through a playlist pre-programmed by the software. Each day, though, for a few hours, a human being sat at the controls. Once a week, on a Friday evening, for two hours, it was Daryl's turn. He clicked-and-dragged songs from one menu to another to create the night's playlist, and he was ready. Daryl's show was the late evening slot: the station's licence meant no broadcasting after ten o'clock at night, so he had two hours to fill until he had to vacate the building and lock up. Instructions from the centre manager were clear: be out of the building, with alarms set and doors locked, as soon as possible after ten o'clock. Classes and clubs were all finished by nine, so Daryl was always on his own for that last hour. Tonight, probably due to the weather, the usual youth club had been cancelled, so it was just Daryl from the start.

The opening jingle announced the start of his show as he shifted the system over from "automated" to "assisted".

'Good evening, locals and lizards. Welcome to this week's Classic Cornucopia of Culture. We've got the usual mix tonight of rock, punk, prog, jazz, blues and even some indie folk to delight and distract. More details later, but for now here's our opener, exploding into the airwaves - "Cherry Bomb" by The Runaways.' The patter was cheesy, cringe-making even, but well-practised and well-worn. The radio DJ persona fitted him like an old leather jacket, the cracks softened and the lining warm and comfortable.

He turned down the volume on the monitor speaker as the drums fired up the post-punk engine. He flicked through his notes, checking back through the radio software to make sure all the evening's tracks were lined up. A couple of minutes later, he segued into The Cars with "Just What I Needed", hurtling through early eighties' New Wave territory.

Through the headphones, Daryl heard a bump. Taking them off, he wondered for a moment whether his imagination had just magnified a bassline or drum fill. He turned off the monitor speaker and listened. Nothing. Only his own breathing and the whirring of the fan inside the computer. Adjusting the faders, he came in just as the track was ending.

'That was The Cars, of course before they went all AOR with asking who's going to drive you home. That was before the days of designated drivers, of course, back in the eighties, even before seat belts were compulsory. It's a wonder we survived such hazards, really. Anyway, from nineteen-eighty-whatever-it-was to much more recent. The masters of murder ballads, here's The Decemberists navigating a different type of hazard. From their album The Hazards of Love, here's "The Rake's Song". If you're driving on your own, turn this one up,' said Daryl, his script improvised on the spot.

The song was about a serial bigamist who kills his wives and children, full of black humour and vaguely disturbing. Daryl had never been married himself. Unlucky in love, he liked to say, but the truth was that he enjoyed being the sole pilot of his own rickety little boat. He felt it was still seaworthy, but for years he had cohabited with his music and the occasional good whisky, and that suited him fine. Besides, there wouldn't be much room for a woman alongside a couple of decades' worth of catalogued, collectible vinyl and scattered, scratched CDs.

An hour passed, Daryl working through his playlist, pausing only to share trivia between songs. By the time he got to the Steven Wilson double bill by way of John Coltrane, Peter Gabriel and The Pretty Things, amongst others, he was comfortable with the way the show was going. No technical hiccups this time. He was talking into a void that may or may not have been listening but certainly wasn't replying. His bladder was pressing, so he put on a nine-minute Marillion album track and left the studio in search of the toilet.

Finishing off, Daryl dried his hands on a paper towel. As he bent to put the used paper in the bin, something fluttered at the periphery of his vision. The bathroom mirror was facing him, so it was entirely reasonable that he had caught his own reflection as he moved. He straightened himself, and looked directly into the mirror. His own reflection. A little haggard, a little tired, a little overweight, but still on the right side of forty and not completely unattractive to women. He still only had one chin and all his own hair, so that was something. The self-appraisal over, it was time to get back to the studio.

Just as he took one step, he heard another footstep on the other side of the door. Then there was another. Someone was in the corridor between the toilet and the studio. 'Right,' he said, and pulled the door as forcefully as he could, intending to take whoever it was by surprise. There was nobody there, of course. 'Fuck's sake,' he admonished himself. 'You twat.' He checked his watch. There were still a few minutes spare until he had to be back in the studio to press another button, so he decided to check the other rooms and make sure no one had come through the front door.

The sound of footsteps, tapping along the vinyl flooring, was coming from upstairs now. The direction was unclear: instead of travelling towards the front or rear of the landing, it seemed to be veering back and forth, fading in one spot to reappear in another. Maybe, he thought, the youth club had been going on after all and some teenagers were left upstairs, doing what teenagers do, probably harmlessly, but possibly not.

Daryl trod carefully. It would be much better to take them by surprise so that they would learn not to mess about in the building after hours. He wasn't planning to be threatening, but potentially making noises about trespassing and calling the police was already filling him with a sense of self-importance that he usually lacked. It was cold outside, but even colder on the top landing. Stark tubes of electric light hummed on the ceiling, the corridor shining in the artificial glare.

Over to Daryl's right was the kitchen, which was locked and in darkness. On his left was the small function room. The door was ajar. He opened it, switched on the light, revealed nothing more than stacked tables and chairs at the edges of the worn carpet. At the end of the cold and clinical corridor were warm shadows, where the extent of the light ended and the entrance to the dance studio began. It was a large mirrored room with a sprung floor, where children's ballet classes and lonely adult ballroom classes would take place. Tonight, the windowless room was dark with shadows that clung to the corners, one shaft of light from the corridor carving a path along the wood laminate floor. It should have been empty, for there was no weight of sound, no shuffle of presence that would betray hidden breathing. There were no signs of life, yet Daryl was not alone.

'All right, you can come out. I'm not going to do anything except ask you to leave,' he said to the darkness.

Daryl felt for a light switch inside the room, flicked it on. Nothing happened. The darkness remained. 'Shit. Must have been tripped,' he said. 'Come on now, I haven't got all night.'

A voice that seemed far distant but also uncomfortably close was singing, almost below the threshold of Daryl's hearing. It was a mellifluous fluctuation of morphemes resembling words, but in no language that he could recognise. The melody was familiar, at once soft and formless but calming and cool. He paused at the doorway, held in that moment. All thoughts left him except the sensation of the faint hint of music wisping across the room. 'What is that?' he asked, breathless.

As Daryl stepped into the thick shadows of the room, a

wave of alarm hit him in the sternum, a heavy bass chord of warning. 'Stay back,' it seemed to say. He clutched his chest, more in surprise than pain. The assertive push of sound still rumbled inside him.

The spray of percussion that lingered in the air spun around his head and formed itself, unseen, into words. Whispering on his shoulder, the voice said, 'Do not echo into the hour. Go. Go now.'

In a daze, Daryl backed into the corridor, and allowed the door to swing shut on the darkness in front of him. A breath of relief settled, like the ending of rain.

The next time he was fully aware of any conscious movement, he was sitting in front of the controls, back in the radio studio. The long progressive rock workout was coming to an end. He added a jingle, which led into him introducing the next song with some trivia about where and when it was recorded, and then the strident riff of Led Zeppelin's "Kashmir" took over. He thought for a moment. What had happened in the last few minutes? It seemed distant and hallucinatory. Had he dozed off at the desk?

It was nearly ten o'clock. Time to sign off and play the last song, click the system over to auto-play, lock up, set the alarm, and leave. It was an easy procedure, one that he had done dozens of times before, if not hundreds. Something from Miles Davis's post-Bitches Brew period closed off the show, and he set about tidying the desk.

As Daryl reached to turn off the monitor, he saw that something was not quite right with the screen. Usually, the playback software showed a playlist of upcoming songs. A random, computer-generated selection, they could range from ABBA to Frank Zappa with anything in between, but this time it was as if the files were corrupted. The names for artist and song were replaced by random, half-formed letters, some of them not even familiar: strange glyphs, almost like runes. Perhaps the software needed an update. That assumption seemed less likely, though, when the music changed.

Through the hazy, crackling monitor speaker, a delicate piano figure was playing. The same notes, quiet but insistent, were repeating: a beautiful phrase in a minor key. Never mind, he thought. Report the glitch in the morning and someone will reboot and apply a fix. Better not mess with it himself. He locked the room and made his way back to the foyer to set the alarm.

The sound seemed to follow him. The repeating piano was joined by additional chords; perhaps it was changing key or there were two instruments playing? It was not coming from a speaker now; it seemed to be filtering down from upstairs. He hadn't imagined it earlier, after all. A low-frequency reggae bassline punctuated his flight up the stairs, terminating in a crash of cymbals as he reached the landing again. The snakelike meandering of an oboe developed the piano lines into a stronger melody, growing louder as he approached the room at the end of the landing.

The air shattered with the screech of distorted guitar as a contorted solo announced his entrance into the dance studio. Runs up and down the neck of the invisible guitar gave way to the choppiness of a punky riff and then a steady rhythm. The room was no longer soaked in

27

shadow. Each note was a bubble of red or pink circling the centre of the room. The harmonic hum of a choir, intoning long vowels, scattered the walls in spotlights of amber. Smears of blue paint streaked across the air with each strum of a guitar string.

Open-mouthed, Daryl squinted into the corners of the room, where it was still grey and indistinct. Colours bounced, reflecting off the ballet mirrors that lined the walls. 'You should not have stayed into this hour,' the colours whispered.

Daryl knew the rule was for him to have vacated the building by now, but surely it was simply an administrative requirement? He came to his senses enough to speak. 'How... Who is that? Who's speaking? Where are you?'

The words were like an arpeggio composed in the very air that he breathed. He felt the reply rather than heard it. 'The beat of the drum. The harmony of voices. The rhythm and tempo of breath and blood. That is where I am, at this hour.'

'I have to go,' Daryl said, backing towards a door that was no longer there. A twelve-bar blues made from smoke and fog settled around, concealing all but an arm's length in front of him.

His father's face, red and angry from so long ago, formed itself from the wisps of solid air. 'What are you listening to? Turn that shit off,' the face said, in a hoarse mockery of the man. Before him flashed the tableau of a teenage Daryl asking his father for guitar or piano lessons. His father laughed. 'Only poofs and drug addicts play guitar, and you're too cack-handed to play a bloody piano. I've got better things to waste my money on,' he said. The laughter loomed over Daryl and he fell to his knees, humiliated and thirteen years old again. He closed his eyes and felt every slap, every kick, every curse, every laugh again and again and again. And through it all, there was music. The radio.

He saw himself, in that moment, as a teenager, lying on his bed, nursing a bruised cheek, wiping tears, and turning up the volume on the radio. Late night sessions with unsigned punk bands a twist of the dial away from jazz trumpet recorded in smoky bars; the weekly chart rundown followed by deep cuts curated by the veteran disc jockey. Music was where he lived, where his misery went to wallow and drown. He would turn the volume up further when the shouting and swearing between his parents overloaded him. When, finally, his father left the family home without a word to his only child, his mother's tears were often the sounds that would keep him awake in the middle of the night.

Daryl was kneeling in the corner of the room now, wreathed in falsetto fog that thinned and dissipated with each incremental slowing of the tempo of the music chiming in his head. Calm now, the crescendo was over and it was reaching its coda.

'What... what are you?' he said.

A diminishing chord replied, 'I am that which was. I was once an ululation over the prairies. I was once a lullaby at the edge of sleep. I was once a marching song leading men into battle. I am the lost music that seeks to be heard. I am the notes that were never played. I am here for you.'

'For me?'

'I have been waiting.'

'Waiting?'

'Waiting to be played.'

'How?'

'You did not go. You are here for me.'

Daryl felt his eyes close with unbidden heaviness. His breathing shallowed. There was a moment of unawareness, an interval in the performance as the music faded.

When he opened his eyes again, he was sitting in a chair, at the desk in the radio studio. The display on the screen showed only one song queuing in the list to be played. The title was indecipherable, random symbols seemingly as placeholders in the software, but the listed artist was clear. Daryl Thomson. His hand hesitated above the mouse; he was sweating. He clicked 'play'.

Outside, the snow had stopped, and the wind was still.

THE SHOP THAT
SOLD TIME

I chthyosaurs once swam where the shop now stood. When the land was drained, sheep were bred there, and men learned to harvest crops. Craftsmen built boats and fished to feed their families. Trade blossomed and communities thrived. Hundreds of years passed and the community became a settlement, then a village, then a town.

On the banks of the river that ran through this Fenland town, grand Georgian townhouses jostled for status alongside the dilapidated old cinema, the poorly-attended Wesleyan chapel, and the Polish supermarket. Between the charity shop that used to be a DVD rental store and the Chinese takeaway, a dark alleyway led to a shopfront shielded from direct sunlight at all times of day.

The hidden shop, tucked away at the end of the cobbled passage, had no name above the door, no painted sign proclaiming its purpose, yet those who knew of its existence knew of it all the same. The proprietor could sometimes be seen tidying and rearranging the items in the window, which ranged from dusty old books to vases of exotic provenance and threadbare rugs with distracting patterns. These things never seemed to find customers, for this was a shop that traded in one commodity only. This was the shop that sold time.

The bell above the door tinkled as David Halliday entered the shop. The man behind the counter looked up from his work, tinkering with the insides of an old carriage clock. He gave the customer a warm smile and beckoned him forward with his screwdriver.

'Good morning, sir. How can I help you today?'

David unwound his scarf and unbuttoned his coat. Sweat beaded on his brow. Securely into his thirties, the cold made him freshly red-faced enough to pass for younger. 'It's warm in here, isn't it?' he said.

'Oh, I don't notice. I don't really feel it. Anyway, welcome to Mister Minuta's Emporium. Feel free to browse.'

David glanced around nervously at the anonymous bric-a-brac on the shelves, and took an unbalanced step towards the counter. He swayed slightly, as if drunk. 'Thank you, but I know what I want.'

Mister Minuta - for that was the name of the elderly man behind the counter - raised his eyebrows. 'I see,' he said. 'A present for your Valentine?'

'No, not quite. Can I sit down?' Without waiting for an answer, David sat heavily on a dining chair that creaked with his weight. Others of its kind were stacked up against the wall, a job lot acquisition waiting to be sold on. His hands trembled as he picked at the threads of his scarf. A stuffed bear, a patchy triumph of taxidermy, loomed beside him, casting a shadow.

'Don't mind Doris,' said the old man. 'She came with

the shop. One of the fixtures and fittings. She's not for sale. Why don't you tell me what brought you here and I'll see if I can help you.'

David rubbed his face, as if trying to wake himself up. 'Well, I feel a bit silly now. You'll probably laugh, but you see I'd never seen this place before or even heard anyone talk about it. So, I was really interested when I met this bloke in a pub. He told me all about your shop and what he bought from you. I didn't really believe it, but he sort of convinced me it was worth finding out.' David laughed, patting Doris on her threadbare furry limb. 'At the very least, it's worth popping in just to meet Doris.'

Minuta took off his reading glasses and rubbed the bridge of his nose. Glasses secured in a little velvet case on his desk, he sat back in his chair. 'Tell me about the man in the drinking establishment,' he said.

'Well, I was drowning my sorrows, as you do,' David began. He blushed and scratched his neck, prickled from the heat of concealing a truth. 'I got talking to this fella about wasted time and wanting… second chances.' He cleared his throat self-consciously before continuing. 'And he told me he'd just come back from a year travelling. Only, he said it wasn't a year. It was more like five. He'd lived it again, over and over, each time going somewhere different. He said he'd bought more time. He said he'd bought it from you.'

The old man nodded. There was to be no mystery here. 'Yes, I'm sure he did. I do indeed offer for purchase some increments of time. But not in the way you probably think, young man.'

'I haven't been called a young man in a while.'

'Well, time is relative, as they say. Many years lie in the grave, and there are many more minutes yet to be born. Years full of regrets, and minutes full of hope.'

David snorted ruefully. 'Yeah, regrets. Got plenty of those.'

'I suppose that's really what you wanted to talk about, isn't it?' There was something about the old man's question that reassured David, that made him feel that this wasn't such a ridiculous situation, and that it was at least worth a shot to be honest with him. At worst, the old man would laugh at David or throw him out, and he would never darken the shop's doorway again.

'Yeah. I've got lots of regrets. I want my time back, I suppose, to fix it. Make different decisions. Have a do-over. Rub out my mistakes.'

The old man flicked the switch on a kettle that nestled between the counter and the wall, and produced two mugs from a shelf beneath. 'Tea?' he said.

'Okay. Why not.'

As the proprietor of the dusty old shop popped teabags into mugs, David began his story. He explained how he had worked so hard for a decade, beginning with losing his job in the first round of austerity cuts, then starting his own business which went bust a few years later during the pandemic. His first wife left him when they lost the house. Fortunately, she had never wanted children, so at least the inevitability of that tug of war was avoided. David had an old schoolmate who pointed him in the direction of a fledgling local company that was looking for a delivery driver. He got on well with the boss, and enjoyed driving around nearby towns, delivering car parts to local garages. It was proper roll-your-sleeves-up work, and he felt good about himself again. It was therefore the perfect time for Nicky to walk into his life. She was an arm around his shoulder and the warmth of a Sunday night. She was his belief and his reason.

One night, she died. And it was his fault.

'Your fault?' said Mister Minuta, handing David a steaming mug of tea. He took it from the counter and returned to his seat. Perching on the edge of the chair, he took a sip and winced. 'I'll let it cool for a sec,' he said.

'You were saying your girlfriend's death was your fault,' the old man resumed. His tone was matter of fact but interested, as if he was taking notes. He sipped his tea, waiting for a reply.

'I was stupid. I was jealous. There was an accident, and if I... hadn't acted in a certain way, I'm sure she'd still be alive. It wasn't my fault, but if I could go back and do something different...'

'Well, you need to understand something first. I can't give you time travel. I'm not entirely sure such a thing would ever be possible in the way that you think about it. But what I can do is let you live the ghost.'

'What do you mean? I don't understand what you're saying.'

'You can't have time back,' the old man said kindly. 'When time has passed, it has died. One year ends and dies, another one is born and begins. What remains is the ghost of that past year.'

'That doesn't make any sense.'

'It does once you realise that ghosts need not be people.

Ghost dogs. Ghost places. Ghost times. An hour can haunt you as easily as the spirit who knocks pictures off the wall in the middle of the night.'

David's tea had grown cold. He set it to one side. 'Well, in that case, how do we do this?'

'You simply have to ask, but be careful. There are rules.'

'Like what?'

'If I give you an hour that you have already lived, an hour that is dead, it has to come from somewhere.'

'Where does it come from?'

'The end of your life. Your friend who says he had five years to live again would have had those five years taken from the end, so his death now comes five years earlier than it would have done otherwise.'

David thought about that for a moment. 'So you know when people are going to die?'

The old man laughed. 'No. What do you think I am, some sort of clairvoyant? No one can see into the future. It hasn't happened yet. I can only deal with ghosts. That's where your notion of time is. In the past, haunting you.'

David stared back, unblinking, his eyes wide as if caught out.

'Tell me what it is that haunts you.'

David took a deep breath, and continued his tale. As David told it, he had seen something on Nicky's phone that had sent him into a rage of jealousy. They were in the car when he confronted her. He was driving, they argued, the vehicle spun out of control. When he regained consciousness, Nicky's body was on the bonnet of the car, surrounded by shattered glass and his screams of horror and regret. The old man listened passively, waiting for

David to finish. Not once did he meet Mister Minuta's eyes whilst he recounted the tragic events.

After a moment, the old man nodded. 'Very well,' he said. 'How much time do you want?'

'I don't know... a year?'

'That I cannot do.'

'Okay,' David paused, frowning. 'Can I go back to that day? I can change what happened that day. Nicky and I can talk instead of getting in the car. Would that work?'

'Well, I can sell you that amount of time if you wish.'

A sigh of relief. 'Okay, then. What will it cost me? What do I have to do?'

'Two months, three weeks and one day. That will be taken from the end of your life. You will die two months, three weeks and one day sooner than you would have otherwise, so that you can relive that day two months, three weeks and one day ago. All you have to do is agree, and when you step outside of the door, you will have the ghost of all that time. You will see your Nicky again.'

'Great, then. I agree.'

The air was warmer when David left the shop. The town was bright with the welcome of Christmas lights, the main street alive with people heading out to eat and drink in the evening. David made his way home, where he knew Nicky would soon arrive from work, tired and flushed, with her phone in her hand.

The first time, David suspected nothing. He had taken her explanations for coming home late from work at face value. She had gone for a drink with Joanna from marketing. It had been really warm in the bar, so that was why she needed a shower as soon as she came in. He only became suspicious when she stayed in the bathroom with her phone. He could hear each notification tone through the door as she carried on a dialogue with someone unseen. They had arranged to meet friends in town later that evening, and they were going to be late. He grew impatient; she seemed tired of him.

This time, David pretended this was all new to him. He accepted her lies about staying late, and didn't interfere with her texting in the bathroom. Instead of complaining and hurrying her along, this time he waited patiently, sitting on the edge of the bed. When she emerged into the bedroom, steam escaping from the bathroom, Nicky saw David waiting. He was tense, his smile forced. She wrapped the towel tight around her breasts and held her phone in its folds. David pretended not to notice.

The first time, David had become suspicious straight away, seized her phone and pushed her onto the bed. He had read her texts. None of them were Joanna from work. They were all from a man who signed himself as Angelo. A foreigner then. There was one about her hair, one about her smile, one about her thighs. There was one thanking her for "earlier". This time, he made no move to intercept the phone. This time, jealousy would not get the better of him.

'What are you smiling at?' Nicky said, blushing.

'You look beautiful,' he replied.

'Well, thank you,' she said, reaching for her hairdryer. 'Now, leave me alone so I can dry my hair. I'll be ready in a minute.'

David paused at the doorway. 'I love you,' he said.

If Nicky said anything in reply, it was drowned out by the roar of the hairdryer.

Last time, they argued. There had been shouting, accusations and denials, but they agreed to put things aside for the evening so that they could meet their commitments to their friends. David had waited downstairs whilst she dressed, trying to control his breathing but allowing his fury to build. In this new version of events, he was calm. He sat on the sofa, scrolling through social media on his own phone. When Nicky came down from upstairs, her perfume arrived before she did, heady and warm. She wore a black dress, smart and classic. Standing by the front door, she pulled on her coat.

'Coming, then?' she said.

'Yep,' David replied, smiling.

In the car, Nicky insisted on driving. The first time, it had been him in the driving seat. He was content now to be a passenger, as he wanted to ensure that the evening ended differently. The first time, she had smiled at a message that appeared on her phone as he turned onto the dual carriageway. David had flown into a rage, assuming the message was from whoever Angelo was. A friend from work apparently, and the texts were jokes, apparently. In trying to grab the bleeping device, David lost control of the steering wheel, Nicky pushed back, and too late he saw the lorry bearing down on them. He swerved away, putting the passenger side directly in the path of the great metal beast. Nicky died on impact. Her phone was cracked beyond repair. David's head spun, but he was unharmed. The guilty survivor, he had sought to alleviate his guilt. Following that quest to the shop that sold time is what led him to this moment, reliving the minutes before the crash would have occurred.

'You know, Nicky…' he began. 'If there's something we need to talk about, I'm all ears. I just…'

'You just what?' she said, irritation showing in her voice as she changed gear.

'I just want you to be happy.' He realised how pathetic it sounded as soon as he said it.

Nicky laughed. 'That right?' she said.

'Listen, Nicky, if you're not happy with me, I…'

'What makes you think that?' The sarcasm was like a knife. He felt the back of his neck prickle and his cheeks burn.

'Nicky…'

She was looking at him now, her eyes not on the road. 'You're pathetic, you know that? Always whingeing, always sad about some woman in your past, always, always… always so bloody boring!'

When she turned back to face the road, the lorry was already inches away. The agonising guttural groan of brakes came too late. Metal punched into metal. The car wrapped around the cab of the lorry like cardboard stiffly enveloping a fist.

The bell above the door tinkled as David entered the shop. Mister Minuta was behind the counter, peering through a magnifying lens at the tiny pieces of a carriage clock that he was repairing. Without looking up, he waved David in.

'Come in,' he said.

David took a seat next to Doris, the stuffed bear. He

waited.

Eventually, the old man put down his screwdriver and glasses. 'Hello again, David.'

'I suppose you've guessed why I'm here.'

'I assume you're thinking at this moment that you can have another try?'

'Well, yeah. Another few weeks off the end of my life, when I'm dribbling in an old folks' home anyway, won't matter that much if I can put things right.'

'Oh, David. That's another assumption. You were never going to live as long as that. Unfortunately, that is only one reason why I cannot help you in that way.'

'What do you mean?'

Mister Minuta came out from behind the counter and stood in front of David, his hands in the pockets of his apron. 'Think carefully, David. What happened after the lorry crashed into the car, with Nicky driving?'

'I... she... Well, it all went black for a bit. Then...' David was confused. He furrowed his brow, trying to recall events since the accident. 'It must be the shock. Suddenly I can't remember anything between the crash and coming here.'

'Yes, indeed.' The old man waited; he nodded understanding.

'What... I mean...'

'We're all ghosts of time here.' Next to David, Doris the bear suddenly seemed warm to the touch. David nodded back. 'This time, David, it was you who died.'

David felt his time ebb away. There was no past, no future, no now. As he closed his eyes and breathed in the emptiness, there was no shop, no land, no sea, and no time.

MOTHER'S DAY

My name is Lilly. This is a story about me and my Mummy. This year, I spent a whole evening making a card for Mother's Day. Daddy came into my room a couple of times: once to bring me a drink and a snack; once to tell me to get into my pyjamas. I'm a good girl, so I got changed quickly. It was really cold in my room, so I had to do a little dance in between having nothing on and pulling on my bottoms. I got my head stuck putting on my top. It was my own fault. I put my big fat head in the wrong hole. Daddy came in and was laughing like a silly monkey while he helped me put it on properly.

After that, Daddy went downstairs to watch telly. I don't know what he was watching but it had screeching brakes and banging and dramatic music on it. Not my kind of thing at all. In the mornings, we watch Peppa Pig together. One time, Daddy laughed so much at something that Daddy Pig said that the milk from his cereal came out of his nose. It made me laugh so much that I nearly did a little wee. I don't think Mummy would ever laugh at the telly, but she would laugh at Daddy. Sometimes, all he would need to do is look at her a certain way and she would crease up, giggling. That's what I think, anyway.

Mother's Day is always a Sunday, so that makes it a

special day. Usually, I spend all day playing with Mummy. She likes to stay with me on Mother's Day and not go out anywhere. Daddy's always busy, so he pops in now and again, but mostly it's my and Mummy's day. He's a good Daddy, so he just gets on with some drilling and sawing and things like that. This year, it was going to be a nice day so I thought we might go out in the garden once Daddy had cut the lawn.

Once I was in my pyjamas, I felt tired so I brushed my teeth, washed my face, and got into bed. Daddy came up and tucked me in. I didn't want a story because I wanted to get a good night's sleep to be up early for Mother's Day. As I closed my eyes, Mummy was there to give me a kiss and say good night.

In the morning, the sun was coming through the gap in the curtains like a river of light. It was early, and Daddy was still asleep. I could hear him snoring all the way across the landing. But Mummy was there, sitting in the little armchair next to my bed. Daddy used to put me down to sleep from that chair when I was a baby. He would give me my bottle, I would fall asleep and he would lay me down gently in my cot. Whenever I woke in the middle of the night, Mummy would come and stop me crying.

'Good morning, Mummy,' I said.

Mummy smiled, wrapping her dressing gown tightly around her. 'Good morning, Lillyflowers,' she replied. I have always liked it when she calls me that. I climbed up onto Mummy's lap and gave her a big hug. 'Happy Mother's Day, Mummy,' I said. I remembered the card I had made her, so I jumped down and grabbed it from my desk, spilling some glitter on the carpet. Mummy laughed.

'Here you are, Mummy.' I handed her the card. On it, I had drawn a picture of me, her and Daddy, all holding hands in the garden. I drew a big shiny sun in the corner of the picture with my best yellow crayon. Everyone was smiling. I tried to make Mummy look especially pretty, and stuck glitter on so that her hair would be all sparkling.

'Oh, thank you sweetheart. That's really lovely,' she said. She was all quiet, as if she was going to cry, but she was smiling so it must have been a good sort of crying.

'I did it all myself.'

'I know. I can tell. You've made it really pretty.'

Every Mother's Day was a day just for Mummy and me. Daddy would do his own thing and we would have fun. Last year, we went for a walk in the woods behind our house. We put on our wellies. Mine were a bit loose because they were new and I was meant to grow into them in no time at all, but they stayed on my feet as we went stomp, stomp, stomp through the woods. Our boots squelched in the mud and we had fun making big sucky footprints. We played hide and seek, but Mummy didn't really hide properly because she knew I would cry if I couldn't find her. It was funny when I could see her arm or leg sticking out from behind the twisty-shaped tree. We collected lots of sticks and branches and made a little den between two trees. All the bits of wood criss-crossed each other just like our fingers when we do a cat's cradle, making a roof. It was only really big enough for me, but Mummy got down on her hands and knees and crawled in with me. It was like a little room of our own in the woods. We pretended one corner was a tiny kitchen, and I served cups of tea and plates of cake made from leaves and twigs. Mummy smiled and sipped at her invisible tea. She gave me a big hug and squeezed me so tightly I thought I was going to pop.

When I was born, it took a long time for the doctors to get me out of Mummy's tummy. I was all shrivelled up like my fingers get when I've been in the bath too long, and I wasn't breathing. They had to use machines to start me up again. Mummy was poorly too, and Daddy said he didn't sleep for nearly three days. I think he made that up to sound silly, because I don't think anyone can stay awake that long. I get sleepy every night before bed, and Daddy sometimes falls asleep in his chair. When he does that, I jump on him and shout, 'Surprise!' Sometimes he's grumpy when I do that; other times he knows it's me and he laughs and tickles me and says, 'Surprise back!'

Mummy likes surprises too, which is why Mother's Day is the best day. I get to give her a card and we play together all day. This year, Daddy came into my bedroom when he had woken up. He rubbed his sleepy eyes and said, yawning, 'What are you doing up so early?'

I said, 'I couldn't wait to give Mummy her card.'

Daddy nodded. 'Want some breakfast?' he asked.

We both said, 'Yeah!' and asked for rice pops and toast and tea and juice. Daddy pretended to write the order down and said, 'Right away, madam.' He went downstairs and started clanging about in the kitchen. I snuggled into Mummy's fluffy dressing gown. 'Are you still cold, Mummy?' I asked.

'No,' she said. 'Not while I've got you for snuggles.'

'Shall we play a game?'

'What do you want to play?'

'Lego!'

Daddy brought us breakfast. Mummy didn't finish her tea but all the toast and rice pops and juice went in our tummies. We made a house and a tower and a boat and a car and a wall with our Lego. I liked mixing up the colours and clicking a brown brick on top of a white one and putting blue and red on top of that one. We would make something, take it apart and then make it again. When I got bored, I said, 'Mummy?'

'Yes, Lilly?'

'Will you read me a story?'

'Yes, of course.'

Mummy sat in the armchair and I climbed up onto her lap. We did all my favourite picture books: stories about naughty squirrels, explorer penguins, greedy caterpillars, little princesses, boys that can't stop burping, and baby monsters lost in the snow. I traced my finger over the best drawings and imagined making new stories with the characters. When Mummy tried to skip over bits she didn't want to read, I knew what was coming next, so I made her read it all. She didn't put silly voices on like Daddy does, but it made me feel all warm and safe just listening to her reading to me.

Just as I was getting tired, Daddy called us downstairs

for lunch. He had made a cheese and tomato pizza. My favourite! I quickly pulled on some leggings and a t-shirt and ran downstairs with Mummy. When we got to the kitchen, she was wearing a nice flowery dress.

'Doesn't Mummy look pretty?' I asked Daddy.

'Well, what do you think?' he replied. He put the plates on the table and some salad. 'Eat your lettuce as well as the pizza,' he said.

'Yes, Daddy,' said Mummy, laughing. It was really fun, sitting at the table, eating pizza. I told Daddy all about our morning playing Lego and reading. He looked as if he was staring somewhere far away inside, but he smiled and said he was glad.

'Can we go out into the garden, Daddy?' I asked.

'Yes, go on then. I'll just do the washing up,' he said. He put the clean unused plate back in the cupboard and put the rest in the sink to wash up after scraping the leftover pizza into the bin.

Out in the garden, the sun was warming the grass that Daddy had just mowed. It had been a bit cold, but it was nicer and sunnier now. Mummy and I played chase around the garden. I found an old football under a hedge, so we did some kicking. I put Mummy in goal against the wall of the garage and scored lots of goals. I think she kept letting me win but I didn't mind.

Afterwards, we sat on the grass with a big cold drink. Daddy was busy washing the car. 'Mummy?' I said.

'Yes, sweetie?' she replied.

'What was I like when I was born?'

'Oh, all shrivelly and squishy. But so yummy I could eat

you all up.'

'Eat me? No, Mummy!'

'Why not? I bet you taste of chocolate and ice cream.' Mummy leaned in and gave me a big tickle, pretending to take big bites out of my neck. It was all tickly and funny and made me giggle.

We stayed outside until it was dinner time. Daddy made us food. I laid the table, putting out three plates, three forks, three spoons: three of everything. Daddy said I was the best waitress ever. After dinner, I went up for a bath. Like we always do, Daddy washed my hair for me. I screamed a bit when the shampoo got in my eye, but he gently washed it away and kissed it better. Daddy always makes everything better. He always knows what to do when I cry. He always hugs the worries away. For a while, anyway. I got all dried off in the fluffiest towel ever. All wrapped up, I went into my bedroom while Daddy rinsed out the bath.

Mummy was waiting for me in the armchair. She was sitting in her dressing gown again, just as fluffy as my towel. She gave my curly hair a rub with the towel, drying it off a bit more.

'Will you help me get in my pyjamas, Mummy?' I asked.

'You're a big enough girl now, Lilly. You can do it yourself. Give me your towel and I'll hang it behind the door to dry,' she said. Her voice was all soft and snuggly.

I put my pyjamas on. Nice and cosy, I climbed into bed. It was starting to get dark, so Mummy turned on my nightlight. Her hair was all curly like mine and smelled of coconut when she leaned in to give me a kiss on the forehead. Her lips were soft and safe and warm. She made everything warm.

'I've had a lovely day, Mummy,' I said, yawning.

'Are you sure? We didn't do much.'

'It's what we do every Mother's Day. Just you and me, playing, being silly and having cuddles. It's the best thing.' I yawned again.

'Oh, you're so tired, poppet.'

'Thank you, Mummy.'

'What for?'

'For being my Mummy today.'

'It's my pleasure.'

'Where will you go when I go to sleep?'

'Oh, you know.'

'Will I dream about you?'

'Maybe. You might. But it's okay if you don't. I'm always looking after you even when you're not thinking about me, aren't I?'

I yawned again. It was getting difficult to keep my eyes open. 'Will Daddy dream about you?'

'He always does.'

'Will I see you again next Mother's Day?'

'You always do.'

'Will Daddy see you next time?'

Mummy looked away for a moment. A little diamond glistened in the corner of her eye. 'He never does.'

'But he lets me spend all day with you.'

'That's because he loves you. It doesn't matter to him whether he can see me or not. It doesn't matter to him whether you seeing me is real or not. He just wants you to be happy.'

'I am happy, Mummy. But I miss you.'

'I know.'

I said, 'Goodnight Mummy,' and then I think I must have gone to sleep, because when I opened my eyes again, it was morning. Daddy was just waking up when I ran into his room and jumped on the bed. I made him jump and we both laughed.

We went down for breakfast. I had rice pops and orange juice, and Daddy had smelly hot coffee. I poked at my cereal with my spoon, making circles in the milk. I wasn't hungry. 'Daddy,' I said.

'Yes, sweetheart?' he replied, sipping his coffee. I think he knew what I was about to ask, because he put his cup down and looked me straight in the eyes, ready to say it again.

'What was it like when Mummy died?'

'Well,' he cleared his throat. 'It was very sad. When you came out of her tummy, you were both very poorly. You got better, but the doctors couldn't fix Mummy.'

'I had a nice day yesterday.'

'I know you did. It was good to see you smiling and laughing. And eating all the pizza,' he laughed.

'Do you see Mummy sometimes like I do?'

Daddy sipped his coffee and didn't answer. His eyes went all shiny.

'Do you dream about her?' I asked.

'I always do,' he said.

THE EASTER HOUSE

When they moved in, the house had not enjoyed being empty, so it welcomed them. At first. The house was built when the coal mines below were young. In time, the house became home to many souls: some filled with love; others empty with loneliness. It rang with life. Dark corners and cold rooms sang death's quiet song when life could ring no more. The house bore witness to all of this for lifetimes. It laughed and wept with the families that filled it with joy and tears.

It was the week before Easter when the removal van rolled up outside the house. It was only their second home together, after three years in a starter home barely bigger than a caravan. A seven-feet-tall hedge hid the lower half of the house from the road, but the drive was wide enough for the van to reverse in. Steven and Abigail Smith had made just enough money on the previous house to be able to make this new one just about affordable. Of course, having been built a century earlier, it was hardly new. But it was new to them. It was the start of a new phase in their lives. Two years into their marriage, this was to be the home that would welcome children and dogs, and laughter and joy.

By the end of the first day, everything had been

emptied out of the removal van. Steven paid them in cash, handing over a little extra so they could have a drink as a thank you for their hard work. His priority was to put the bed together; Abigail covered it with fresh sheets and a new duvet. They fell into bed earlier than usual, as they were yet to get any signal connected to the television and unpacking all the basics to be able to eat, drink and sit down was exhausting enough. They slept without curtains and awoke to the first rays of dawn and the twinkling greeting of birds.

'Good morning, Mrs Smith,' said Steven, as he rolled out of bed. 'Tea?'

'Obviously. And toast,' Abigail replied.

'If I can find the toaster. Looking at it, I'm not sure I can trust the grill.'

'Not until we've had it cleaned anyway.'

'Not going to clean it yourself? Are we getting somebody in?'

'Are you going to do it?'

'Nope.'

'We'll get that oven cleaner bloke in, then. Didn't you notice the previous owners left old pans in the oven?'

'Eww. Fair enough. I'll get that tea.'

'Snap to it, then.' Abigail slapped his thigh and turned over to snuggle back down into the new duvet.

Steven trailed his hand along the bannister as he walked downstairs, smiling to himself. Things were coming together. They both had good jobs, Abigail was becoming even more beautiful as she entered her thirties, and they now had a proper house that they could add value to. A mirror left by the previous owners was at one end of the landing, making it seem bigger. As he passed it, he caught his own reflection out of the corner of his eye. Not bad. Could do with a few more hours in the gym, a good shave and some decent pyjamas. His boxer shorts and t-shirt combo wasn't the sexiest, he knew that.

On the stairs, a long vertical window reached to the ceiling of the first floor. Set into sections of it were various colours of stained glass, a faux antique look that made Steven cringe. Still, it cast wandering diamonds of red, green and blue on the staircase as sunlight struck the glass. In the kitchen, Steven filled the kettle, clicked it on, and popped tea bags into mugs. As he waited for the water to boil, he looked out at the garden, overgrown with weeds. It was a long, meandering garden, a legacy of a time when planners were generous with building plots. At the end were an old shed and a dilapidated greenhouse. Both had seen better days.

'Can't wait to get at them with a hammer,' Steven mused. He imagined a nice, wooden summerhouse replacing the sagging structures, he and Abigail sitting on cushions late into the evening, drinking wine and looking up at the stars. Maybe with a toddler and a puppy playing at their feet. But first things first. Tea.

'You'll have to have it without milk,' Steven said, placing a mug beside the bed next to Abigail.

She opened one eye. 'Why?'

'Milk's off.'

'Oh yeah. We need to buy a fridge.'

'That we do.'

Steven wriggled back into bed next to Abigail, scraping his foot against her calf. 'Oi! That's cold!' she exclaimed.

Steven giggled, sipping his tea. No milk. Yuck.

'You're such a child,' she said.

The morning was fraught with drilling, hammering, assembling furniture, hanging curtains; the afternoon involved a trip to dispose of bags of rubbish that seemed to be generated from thin air. The evening, when it came, was host to a takeaway and a bottle of wine.

'I met the neighbours earlier, when you went to the tip,' said Abigail, in between sips of her pinot grigio.

'Next door?'

'Yep. Albert and Joy. In five minutes, I got the whole story. They're in their seventies, they've lived here since they got married, before the invention of nostalgia. Albert gave me the skinny on the previous owners. According to him, they used to grow weed in that shed at the end of the garden.'

'No wonder they were so chilled out.'

'Seriously, though, I hope not. Have you tested the burglar alarm yet?'

'Not yet. I'm a bit nervous of it. Previous owners were a bit overzealous. There's sensors on every window, every outside door, movement sensors in every room, and there's even a couple of them in the garden. Maybe they were protecting the marijuana farm in the shed.'

Abigail snuggled in closer to Steven on the sofa, shouldering in for protection. 'Well, there's none there now. Is there?'

'Plenty of other weeds in the garden, but not that kind. I'll set the alarm when we go to bed, then we'll see if it works.'

She looked up at him with a smile. 'Better go and do

it now, then.' A kiss followed, a whispered promise, and an understanding between husband and wife. As Abigail changed upstairs for bed, Steven locked doors and keyed a four-digit code into the house alarm system. He turned off the lights and joined Abigail upstairs.

Sleep was a pleasant miasma, swimming in the warmth and dreaming of dreams of nothing. Steven was ripped into sudden consciousness by a midnight blare of sound, filling the air with urgency.

'What's going on?' mumbled Abigail, eyes still closed in the darkness.

'Bloody alarm. I'll see what's going on and turn it off,' Steven replied, suddenly alert.

He took the stairs two at a time. Something blurred at the corner of his eye but he quickly dismissed it. In the hallway, he turned off the alarm and noted which zone had been activated. Outside.

In his bare feet and boxer shorts, he stepped onto the lawn. In the darkness, a shape was moving in the greenhouse. Steven ran towards it, his heart thumping in his throat. The shape moved out of the shadows, growing arms and legs.

'Get out of my garden!' was all Steven could think to shout.

The hooded shadow ran across the lawn and clambered over the back fence to be lost in the night behind. With the security lights now shining, Steven could see a boot print in the border at the base of the fence, from where the intruder had launched his escape. He swung around to see the shed door hanging open. The padlock had been forced open, and sundry contents were randomly strewn across the lawn. None of the various tools, bits of wood and buckets were seemingly what the intruder had been seeking, having been abandoned on the grass.

When the police came at lunchtime, the two female officers were sympathetic but pessimistic. Her ponytail scraped so tightly that her forehead seemed stretched like cellophane, PC Hayley Jeffs took a couple of photographs of the bootprint. 'This probably won't do much. We've given you a crime number, so at least you can claim on the insurance for any losses,' she said.

'I don't think much, if anything, is missing. Just some damage that I can probably fix myself. But that's not the point,' Steven replied.

'I suppose it's a good thing we've got that alarm,' said Abigail, handing PC Jeffs and her silent colleague a cup of tea each.

The police woman smiled the smile of someone withholding secret information. 'Yes, well, I should think the previous owner had it as a preventative measure, given that there's a bail hostel up the road.'

'What?'

'Yeah. They often pay the neighbours a visit when they run out of cash.'

'Great.'

Steven said, 'Next Door said he thought the previous owner used to grow weed. Maybe that's what he was looking for. I'm almost sorry to disappoint him.'

Sipping her tea, Hayley Jeffs nodded sagely. 'Well, we haven't seen any evidence of that here, so I doubt they'll come back now. Unless you've got some squirrelled away in the attic.'

'Ah, well, you're welcome to look up there. It's only a little hatch so I haven't even been up there myself yet. I assume it's empty. Apart from the mad first wife, of course.'

Hayley laughed. She knew he was joking, but missed the literary reference. The officers drained their tea, finished off the paperwork, and left Abigail and Steven to clear up the minor mess on the lawn.

That evening, as Steven and Abigail were arranging books on to shelves, Abigail paused in front of an alcove next to the stone fireplace. 'That's weird,' she said, shivering involuntarily.

'What is?' Steven was half listening, leafing through his rediscovered copy of an old paperback.

'Look at my arms.' Steven turned to look at Abigail. Her bare arms were gooseflesh. 'This spot. Just here. It's absolutely freezing.'

Steven was mere feet away, and he was comfortably warm. It was average weather for Easter, nothing remarkable either way. He stepped over to be beside his wife. His hand grew suddenly cold as he moved to touch her arm, as if reaching into a refrigerator. Testing a theory, he extended his arm towards the ceiling, circling Abigail. 'That really is weird,' he said.

'I know. I don't like it.'

'It's like there's a... column of air colder than the rest of the room. What's above it?'

'That's the spare bedroom. It's where that damp smell is. I thought it was just the old carpet. We're going to replace them anyway, so I didn't really think much about it. But it's only in that spot, like a...'

'Column of air?'

'What's in the attic above it?'

'I don't know. We haven't been in there yet. Maybe there's a draft from a hole in the roof or something. Can't be much, or the survey would have shown it up. I'll check it out tomorrow when I've got a bit of daylight. Sun's gone down now.'

Abigail shivered. She sought refuge on the sofa. Pulling on her fleece, she assumed a mock horizontal position like a Roman emperor, reclining and gesturing for the services of a slave. 'I will now have food, wine, and I will doomscroll on my phone until it's time for bed.'

Steven laughed, and went into the kitchen to throw some pasta together. Full of carbohydrates, tomato sauce and cheese, they sipped their wine together until Abigail fell asleep, her head on Steven's lap. The sitting room was comfortable now: the familiar tokens of their lives had positions; it was starting to really feel like home. But something was not yet quite right. He stared at the alcove. As he tried to adjust his gaze to the area that had been so cold earlier, he lost focus. He blinked, as if to reset his vision. What he had described as a cold column of air seemed almost to have a different texture to the rest of the room. He blinked again.

'I'm tired, that's all it is,' he said to himself.

'What?' Abigail groaned. His voice had woken her.

'Time for bed,' he said.

When the alarm went off this time, it was past midnight, well into the depths of those early hours that are neither night nor morning. The glaring noise drowned out all other senses until Steven tapped in the code. This time, the sensor that had sent the alarm sounding was in the living room. He turned to look down the hall. The door to the living room was half closed, not as he had left it. In the gloom, the room beyond was grey and black, the shapes of night blocking and looming.

Steven felt for a light switch, and flipped it on. The bulb popped. Darkness remained. Abigail called down from upstairs, 'What happened?'

'Bulb went. It probably tripped. Whole place needs rewiring, probably,' he replied.

Feeling through the shadows, he opened the door further. Everything in the living room was made of night, moonlight seeping through the blinds. Steven's eyes were drawn towards one corner of the room, where the air was cold. In front of the alcove, the meagre light seemed to bend around something shapeless and dense that hung between the floor and ceiling. He stepped towards it, and it was gone.

'What are you staring at?' It was Abigail's voice, behind him. She had followed him downstairs.

'It was nothing.'

Abigail flicked on the overhead light. Everything in the room was mundane and stark in the brightness from the bare bulb. 'Oh, turn that off. Too bright,' Steven said.

'You'd better put that shade on it then. Better yet, we could buy a nice light fitting.'

'Dream on, You know I'm shit at electrics.'

'Come on, let's go back to bed. And leave that bloody alarm turned off. It's useless.'

Following Abigail, Steven glanced back at his shoulder

at the invisible cold nothing of the living room. The sway of her body under her nightdress led him upstairs to warmth and whispered endearments in the comforting dark.

Over the next couple of days, with some time before they had to resume the routine of working for a living, they set about getting the house in order. Hanging curtains, building flat-pack furniture, painting woodwork, cleaning neglected cupboards, were all part of the circus that gradually turned a house into a home. There were no further visitors, solid or shadowy, and the alarm was deactivated. Steven decided it was too much trouble for now.

Two days before Good Friday, Steven was on his back, wrench in hand, tightening a new waste pipe under the kitchen sink, when he sensed Abigail standing beside him. He pulled himself out from a halo of pipes, buckets and bottles of bleach to see his wife wiping tears from her face, her hair tied back in a ponytail over jeans and t-shirt flecked with paint. She was holding a plastic stick as if it were something broken, delicate, fragile. 'It's negative,' she said.

Steven paused, unsure what was the best thing to say. When they had talked about trying for a baby, it existed in the distant future for him. He had no expectation that anything would happen yet, and he barely thought about it beyond it being a vague possibility. He was not plagued by dreams of being a father.

'Aren't you going to say anything?' Abigail insisted.

'Oh, Abi. I'm sorry. We'll keep trying.' He started

getting to his feet.

'Keep trying?' She threw the pregnancy test at the kitchen bin. It bounced off the rim and clattered to the floor. 'We've been trying for six months!'

'I know...' he began, but she had already backed out of the kitchen.

In the living room, Abigail perched on the sofa, one hand clutching her forehead, the other clenched into a tight fist. Steven knelt before her, placed his hands on her knees, leaning his face close to hers. 'Abi,' he said, helplessly.

She cried quietly. He waited, cheek pressed against hers, arms now around her.

When the crash came, it took Steven a moment to register. In the second that it took him to realise that the sound had originated from above, the window had already shattered on the ground outside.

He took the stairs two at a time. He took the turn at the top of the staircase. He took great strides into the spare bedroom, where the door hung off its hinges. His eyes travelled to the bed, where the freshly made duvet was disturbed with an indentation, as if a body had launched from there to the open window.

The window was not open. It was, in fact, absent. Complete with frame, the double-glazed unit had crashed to the ground outside. Masonry crumbled at the edges where the window had been. Something had forced the door back against itself. Something had thrown its weight onto the bed. Something had blown out the window.

Catching up with him, Abigail gasped. 'What - I mean,

what,' she began.

'It's like… it couldn't be the wind. Nothing else is open. Even if it blew through the bathroom window, it would have to turn left and then right. Wind doesn't work like that.'

'The window… How?'

Steven had no answer. He moved over to the side of the bed, where the strange, musty smell was stronger than ever, even with gusts of air washing the dust back in from outside.

The rain began whilst Steven battled to board up the gap with inadequate tools, flimsy wood and his own lack of manual dexterity. With its temporary protection against the elements screwed into place, the room was calm and still that afternoon. As Steven was packing his tools away into the metal toolbox he had inherited from his father, Abigail came in with a cup of tea.

'Thanks,' he said. They both sat on the edge of the bed, sipping tea and staring at the indentation in the duvet that they had yet to smooth out.

'Am I going to say it, or you?' said Abigail.

'It couldn't have been another one of those thugs from the bail hostel. We'd have seen or heard him break in, and he'd have landed with the broken glass. Besides, why would they do that? Seems a strange way to try and nick stuff.'

'No,' she sighed. 'You know what I mean.'

Steven could barely contain a laugh. 'You mean a ghost?'

She nodded. Her eyes showed she was serious.

'Well, it is weird, but there's got to be an explanation.

It's an old house. There's bound to be bits falling apart.'

'The double glazing isn't that old.'

'Yeah, well, it's not a ghost. No such thing.'

That night, they slept with the lights on downstairs and the alarm system switched off. Doors and all the remaining windows were locked, bulwarks against the outside world and its garden invaders. Abigail fell asleep with her head on Steven's chest, and he lay awake listening to the rain and his own breathing. The move to this house was meant to be the next step in their marriage: they had made enough on their first house for the mortgage to be comfortable and for them to be able to afford taking a chance on starting a family. Steven and Abigail had the next few years clearly planned out, at least in principle, and it all involved this house and a child. It had only been a few months, but Abigail had decided now was the time, and each month brought with it disappointment when she realised that she was not yet pregnant. Steven was more sanguine: if it happened, it happened; if not, well, kids were not everything. But he did like the idea of being a Dad. He had already started constructing a persona for himself of bad jokes, poor football skills, professional-level Lego-building abilities, and avoiding changing nappies. How much the reality would be shaped by the fantasy was yet to be determined.

In the sleeping darkness, he stared up at the ceiling. Sooner or later, he would have to venture into the loft. There was no ladder, so he would have to drag one up out of the shed. The pitched roof meant that there wouldn't be much in the way of standing height, so he was only expecting to be able to shove a few boxes up there. Inwardly, he laughed at himself for his nervous reluctance to explore part of his own house, but he thought of the strange hallucinatory coldness in the living room, the imagined presence directly above it in the spare bedroom, and whatever could be above that in the void of the roof.

Gradually, he drifted off to sleep. When he awoke, sunlight was streaming in, and Abigail was downstairs clinking mugs and teaspoons. Steven threw on some clothes and joined her in the kitchen.

'We still need to buy a fridge,' she said, handing him a black tea.

'Oh yeah. Should've done that yesterday. Not quite Easter yet. Could pop out and do that today. I'm enjoying this week, just you and me, pottering about in our new house. It'll be weird going back to work.'

'Yeah. You, me and our haunted house.'

'It's not haunted, Abi.'

'Yeah? Albert and Joy from next door might beg to differ.'

'In what way?'

'While you were in bed, they knocked on the door. That's what woke me up. They wanted to know if we needed anything, which was nice of them. Anyway, I couldn't shift them off the doorstep once they got started about the previous owners again.'

'More revelations? Meth lab in the greenhouse? Human trafficking in the garage?'

'Not quite. There was a baby who died here though, in the house.'

'Oh, that's sad.' Steven started opening cupboards,

looking for bread to put in the toaster. 'Are we out of bread as well?'

'Listen,' Abigail said, grabbing his hand. She was suddenly serious, a softness in her eyes as he turned to face her. She pulled her cardigan around her torso tightly, as if suddenly cold. 'It wasn't the previous owners. They were divorcees, second marriage, grown-up kids, moved out to a flat. They were older than us, even if they were drug dealers. Remember they were a bit shady about why they were moving, after only living here for a year or so?'

'Well, yeah, but not our problem. I'd have more of a bone to pick with them about not telling us about the bail hostel up the road, to be honest. Have we got anything for breakfast at all?'

Abigail closed the cupboard door and shoved a packet of biscuits into his chest. 'There! Eat that. Now, will you listen to me?'

'Sorry.' Steven dunked a digestive biscuit in his tea and took a bite. 'Go on, my absolute love.'

She almost smiled. 'Don't take the piss. Listen, this baby the neighbours were talking about: they said it died here, in the house. Stillborn.'

'Oh, that's awful.'

'Guess where?'

'You're not going to tell me it was in the living room?'

She nodded. 'Right where that cold spot is.'

'That still doesn't mean…'

'And, afterwards, the mother bled to death in the bedroom above the sitting room. She fell by the bed.'

'By the bed? Bullshit.'

'No, it's true. At least, that's what they said. I didn't tell them about the cold spot or the weird smell. Apparently, the husband was so devastated he just left. The house was left empty for years.'

'They didn't include any of that in the estate agents' details, did they?'

Steven looked out the side window at the neighbours' house, which was mostly hidden by bushes and a tree that loomed over the top of the fence that separated the two properties. From what he could see, nicotine-stained net curtains hid a quiet, still interior. 'I haven't even seen the neighbours yet.'

'Maybe they only speak to me because they can see how anti-social you are.'

They both wanted to keep busy for the rest of the day. Finally, a local firm replaced the window for them at short notice. The insurance company was suspicious until Steven emailed them some photographs with which they could not argue, and they covered it. They bought a fridge, plugged it in and filled it with provisions. The house gradually came together in the way they wanted it. Abigail went out to meet some girlfriends for a drink. Steven dropped her off, was happy to pick her up safely afterwards, and watched television in between. They were happy, the house was calm, and each day was a routine of unpacking, hanging pictures, and decorating. Still, both Steven and Abigail were reluctant to venture into the attic. It felt almost as if it was willing them not to. Each time Steven decided to grab a ladder and open the hatch, something else distracted him or some other job reared its head.

Good Friday arrived, the beginning of the Easter

weekend, and another few days they planned to spend together, knowing that they were going back to work after the bank holiday. Parents were angling for invitations to the house, but both Steven and Abigail were putting that off, allaying parental judgement for at least another week. In the afternoon, they took the car to the supermarket to buy another week's food, which in their case mostly consisted of wine and microwave ready meals, but at least they had a working fridge now.

With a boot full of shopping, Abigail pulled on to the drive just as sprinkles of rain were dotting the ground. Just as Steven was climbing out of the car, Abigail halted him. 'Is it me,' she said, 'or is the side door open?'

'Wait here,' Steven replied. 'I'll check.'

Sure enough, the side door into the kitchen had been forced. The lock on the PVC door was hanging loosely. He stepped in, taking care not to make any noise. He held his breath, in case the sound of his own breathing would confuse his senses as he listened for any sound inside the house. A clump and a scrape of metal against wood echoed through the ceiling. Adrenalin surging, he had run upstairs before it even occurred to him to call out to Abigail.

A stepladder - his own, in the house from decorating the day before - was positioned beneath the loft hatch on the first floor landing. The hatch had been opened and pushed to one side. Dangling from it was a pair of skinny legs in torn, faded jeans and a pair of dirty boots.

'What the fuck!' was all that Steven managed to articulate before the intruder became aware of him and started to lose his footing on the stepladder.

The skinny legs buckled to the floor as the ladder tumbled away. The legs were followed by a skinny torso in a thin t-shirt and the face of a scared teenager.

The boy got to his feet, tried to dance past Steven, who blocked his path on the landing. 'Sorry!' he said. 'I'm sorry!'

Steven's panic was dissipating as he saw his intruder, to be replaced by bubbling righteous anger. 'What the fuck are you doing?' he demanded.

'Sorry! I said I'm sorry!' The boy had his hands up as if surrendering. A sports bag, empty except for a crowbar, was at his feet. He was reaching for it.

'Don't you dare. Abi!'

Abigail's voice came from the hall below, as calm as he needed it to be. 'On it!' she called up, and began talking into her phone. She must have got concerned when Steven failed to come straight back out and followed him in. 'The police are on their way!' she added.

'Shit. I'm sorry!' said the teenager, his eyes wide with panic.

'What were you looking for?' persisted Steven, blocking his only route of escape.

'Weed, innit. Let me go, please!'

'For fuck's sake, haven't you worked out we haven't got any?'

'I know, I know!' His panic was escalating. He glanced back up at the loft hatch, as if afraid of something up there.

'What's up there?'

'Nothing. I didn't get in. You stopped me. Please let me go!' Ducking his head, he pushed into Steven's side.

Unbalanced, Steven fell against the wall as the boy turned on to the stairs.

Already stepping into the hall from outside was PC Hayley Jeffs. She looked up at the young burglar coming down. 'Oh, Liam,' she said, with a note of resigned disappointment.

The boy's shoulders slumped and he sat at the foot of the stairs, giving up.

The policewoman pulled him to his feet and handed him to her partner, who smiled when she also recognised the miscreant. With Liam safely stowed in the police car outside, Hayley concluded the formalities with Steven and Abigail. 'Yes, you've probably guessed that this young man is known to us. And yes, he's on bail.'

'For burglary?' Abigail guessed.

'Got it in one.'

'Almost definitely he was hoping he'd find some plants or even better some actual drugs, and sell them on. Forensics will be round later, so be careful what you touch. But we've got him bang to rights, as they say. He's just a chancer, a bit of an opportunist, our Liam. Once word gets round there's nothing worth nicking here, you'll be fine.'

'Charming.'

'Be thankful for small mercies.'

The 'forensics team' turned out to be an overweight admin person with some brushes and a too-tight t-shirt. Once he had finished, Steven stood on the landing, eyes fixed on the ceiling hatch. Abigail stood next to him, arms folded.

'I'm fed up with this,' she said.

'I know. Do you want to move? I know we've only been here a week, but if it freaks you out...'

She gave him a withering glance. 'No. This is our home. If we get another break-in, I'll beat him to death with my shoe. Just not one of my good ones, obviously.'

Steven looked at her with more desire than ever. Her resolve and refusal to take any shit was the sexiest thing on the planet. His gaze swivelled back to the hatch. 'I'm going up there,' he said.

'What, now?'

'Yep.'

'About bloody time. I'll get the torch.'

The air in the attic was still, warm, stale, as if it had been preserved for years. Dust coated his nostrils with every breath. The pitched roof offered no height where he could stand, and it was impossible to see whether any of the space was boarded beneath the rolls of thick insulation. Where it had been unrolled, the lack of light made nothing discernible beyond a few feet. The flash of the torch could not reach the corners, and there was no light switch. A blinking panel and a tangle of wires was over to Steven's left elbow, evidently a hub of some sort for the alarm system. The water tank bubbled behind him. He swept across the scene with the torch, bit by bit, trying to ascertain shapes and shadows. He stopped. There was something.

The yellow oval of the torchlight fell on a basket, nestled in the loft insulation. It was a Moses basket, a wicker bassinet that once held a baby. It was in one of the furthest corners of the roof space, directly above the spot in the spare bedroom with the musty smell, itself directly above the cold column of air in the living room. Shadows hid the inside of the basket. If it held anything now, it was unseen in the darkness and out of reach.

Steven leaned forward, tested his weight. He could not be sure that crawling across would not end in him crashing through the ceiling. There was no way to tell whether there was firm footing under the insulation. His hand shook, causing the torch to rattle. His feet were unsteady on the stepladder. Abigail steadied his ankle with her hand.

'You okay?' she asked. 'Can you see anything?'

Steven hesitated. He went over the possibilities quickly. He could tell her what he saw, and confirm once and for all that something very strange was going on, in which case he would either have to retrieve it or they would move out. Neither was a good outcome. He needed time to consider. 'No, nothing,' he said. 'Just insulation and cobwebs.'

Later, whilst they cooked dinner together, Abigail stirred the sauce whilst Steven took a bottle of white wine out of the fridge. 'I'm just popping to the loo,' she said, passing him the spoon. He took over the gentle motion of stirring, enjoying the process of cooking in partnership. After a minute or so, he turned down the heat and opened a drawer, looking for a corkscrew.

'Abi! Where's the corkscrew? It's not in the drawer,' he called.

The reply came from the doorway. Abigail was already back from the toilet. 'We might not need it. At least, I won't be having any wine,' she said.

Steven turned to see her in the doorway, her cheeks

flushed, her eyes glistening, and her lips unable to conceal a smile. She held a plastic stick in her hand. 'Happy Easter,' she said. 'I'm pregnant.'

The following morning, Steven was on the front drive, trimming the overgrown hedge that separated his and Abigail's house from Albert and Joy next door. Through a gap in the foliage, he noticed a familiar car pull up on to the neighbours' drive. It was the car belonging to Delia, the estate agent who had been so helpful in making sure that their sale went through. He decided to pop round to the front of the drive to say hello.

'Oh hello, Steven,' said Delia, straightening her suit jacket. Her heels were a little unsteady on the gravel, so she steadied herself against the car.

'Just thought you'd like to know, after a couple of hiccups, we've settled in nicely. Although maybe there is something I should tell you about.'

'Well, that would be lovely. I've just got to do a few things first.'

'Are Albert and Joy selling their house as well, then?'

Delia looked confused. 'Um... yes, their son is finally putting the house on the market. I'm here to take some photos and measurements. How did you... Did you know them?'

'Well, Abi has spoken to them. I haven't yet. It seems all quiet and closed up there.'

'I'm not surprised. Are you sure your wife has spoken to them?'

It was Steven's turn to be confused now. 'Uh... yeah. Why?'

'Well, we can only sell it now because probate has just come through. They both died about a year ago, just a few weeks apart.'

SPRING RAIN

On the twenty-fourth day of May 2019, Theresa May resigned as Prime Minister. At the start of the month, she had fired her Secretary of State for Defence for leaking confidential information relating to national security. It was only one of many examples, so many more yet to come, of the revolving door of British politicians being allowed in and out of Parliament, seemingly with impunity and without consequences. Mississippi floods and Indian Ocean cyclones; armed conflict in Afghanistan, Gaza, Pakistan, Syria, Nigeria; gunmen burning down a Catholic church; so much death. A television show was cancelled when a guest committed suicide; lies and untruths became the currency of the day.

On the day of Theresa May's resignation, US President Donald Trump sent troops and missiles to the Persian Gulf just in case a war with Iran happened; abortion was banned in a US state; twenty children died in a fire in India; a bomb filled with bolts killed people in Lyon; and a man stood on the edge of a bridge, waiting for rain.

The man had planned to kill himself that evening. The weather forecast had said it would start raining at eight o'clock; he had intended to jump so that he could feel the downpour around him as he fell into the waters below.

He had not counted on a passing motorist stopping to help him.

The woman had finally left her husband that evening. She drove away from the house in his car, with her bags packed. She intended to drive on through the rain that was forecast, with no particular destination in mind. She was just going to go. She had not counted on stopping to help a man on a bridge.

The sun was setting: the warmth of the day still lingered. The bridge reached over a dual carriageway, but was itself little more than a two-lane side road used to reach a fishing lake on the other side. It was therefore never very busy come evening. The man had walked from where he abandoned his car. Police would find it listing in a ditch the following morning, streaked with mud and scraped with damage from ploughing into a hedge. They would find that the car was registered to Manson James, an unremarkable marketing copywriter for a packaging firm. He had recently been made redundant, the unintended consequences of the UK's exit from the European Union already starting to bite at the ankles of unremarkable people such as him. Now, he stood on the outside of the guard rail, holding on but looking down at the busy traffic below.

Clouds were gathering: the chill of the evening was coming. Half way along the bridge, the woman's car had parked. The road was quiet, and no other traffic had to negotiate the obstruction as she gripped the steering wheel, tense and nervous. Police would be searching for the car in the morning, but for now it ticked over quietly on the bridge. The car belonged to her husband, but it was Emilia Nowak who was driving. She and Piotr had moved to England ten years ago, and were now so settled that neither of them really thought of themselves as Polish anymore. They considered themselves to be European, and comfortable as part of England. It was home. Their children were born in England. Now, though, she sat in Piotr's car, staring at the man who looked as if he was about to jump to his death.

Emilia turned off the engine and climbed out of the car. She locked the door behind her and put the keys in her jeans pocket. It had been warmer earlier, but now she was dressed for whatever may come. She zipped up her hoodie. Ensuring that she stayed a few steps away so that she would cause no alarm, she hesitated for a moment. When she was sure that the man had sensed her presence, she spoke.

'Hello?' Emilia said. 'Are you okay?'

Manson could hear her, but stayed in position, his knuckles whitening as his grip tightened on the rail. 'Yes thanks,' he replied.

'I mean, do you need some help? It doesn't seem safe.'

His laugh was hollow. 'Ha, well, life isn't safe.'

Reflecting on her own experience, she had to agree. 'I know what you mean,' she said. 'Why don't you climb back over this side and we can talk about it?'

'Just leave me alone. You don't know me. I don't know you. We don't owe each other anything. Just go.'

'I can't really do that.'

'Why?' For the first time, Manson turned to face her. In the diminishing light, his eyes stood out to her against his skin. She felt pale and dun next to him. Slightly younger than him, he seemed no different from any other man that she encountered day to day, just, she had to acknowledge, slightly more attractive. She briefly wondered how such a handsome man could find himself in such despair.

'I... well... I suppose now that I'm here, I would feel responsible for what happens to you if I leave now.'

'Well, you're not.' Manson looked at her now. Slender, short-haired, athletic. No. Undernourished rather than athletic. She had a nice smile, one of those that shows some intelligence, unlike the fake smiles most people put on.

'My name is Emilia,' she said, extending her hand and then quickly withdrawing it when his grip tightened further on the rail.

'Good for you. Let me be, Emilia.' His eyes glistened.

'What's your name?' she insisted.

He sighed, as if bothered by an irritating child. 'Manson,' he said.

'I'm pleased to meet you, Mister Manson.'

He rolled his eyes. 'No, Manson is my first name.'

'Oh. Sorry.'

'I get it all the time.'

There was a moment of silence as Emilia considered what she could say to help him. She envisaged him leaping from the edge of the bridge at any second, and she wanted the image out of her head. Manson turned back to stare blankly at the roar of the road beneath, sprinkled with lights.

Finally, she said, 'Perhaps I can help you?'

'What, are you some kind of drive-by psychiatrist cruising the roads looking for patients?' He laughed, but there was no humour in it.

'No, but I did study psychology in Poland. For a year, before my husband decided he wanted to move here.'

'That worked out well then.'

'Well...' she shrugged.

'Nothing you can do for me. Leave me alone.'

'Try me.'

Manson's shoulders slumped, and he adjusted his position. His back was hurting. He was on secure footing, but he had to keep leaning backwards to avoid tipping forward. He wasn't ready yet. Perhaps if he indulged the woman, he might be able to relax enough to think clearly. He wanted his mind to be peaceful and clear before he jumped. He had to be ready.

'Go on then.'

Emilia blushed. Now she had to follow through with something but she was afraid she might say the wrong thing and he would jump anyway. If that were the case, she reasoned, it would matter very little what she said. She decided to be direct.

'Everybody's life is a little bit... rubbish. Why is yours rubbish today, Manson?'

This time, his laugh was genuine. 'That question on its own is enough to make me jump. Ha. Okay, you want to know? Well, I lost my job because I spoke up when I saw my manager falsifying accounts. It got turned on me. Turns out no one is interested in what's right, just what's easy. Then my girlfriend dumped me. We were going to get married next year. That was probably my fault too.

I can't afford the rent on my own. I've been sleeping in my car. I thought I had everything sorted out. I was wrong. I've got no family; none of my so-called friends are interested; I can't get a job or claim benefits as I'm on the street; no hope, no future. That enough for you?'

Emilia hesitated. Her mouth might have dropped open. She struggled to find something to say. 'I-I'm sure you're a good person...' she began.

The first drops of rain came. Manson angled his face upwards to feel the water sprinkle his face. He then looked down to stare blankly at the road below, now dark in the encroaching evening. 'That isn't enough,' he said. His hands opened and he tipped forward, nothing holding him back. Before Emilia could react, he was gone into the darkness below. A heavy crunch of bone and metal followed a screech of brakes.

Bewildered, Emilia wandered back to her car through the rain. Retrieving her mobile phone from the passenger seat, she took a calming breath. She tapped the screen. The one percent of battery power that remained allowed it to flicker into life for a second, but it was a digital death rattle. With no way to contact anybody, Emilia glanced desperately in both directions along the bridge. The road was silent, the emptiness like a cruel parent withholding comfort. In the car, she pressed her forehead against the steering wheel, still too shocked to register how to respond. The man had killed himself. She could have stopped him, but she failed. It may as well have been her who pushed him. But she had to let someone know she was there, and explain to the police what happened.

She started the car. As it coughed into life, her trembling hands tried and failed to clip in her seating belt. When the car began to accelerate, her eyes were too full of tears to notice that she was on the wrong side of the road. The thickening onslaught of rain obscured her view of the bend in the road and the low stone wall. When the figure of a woman, thin and hunched in the rain, appeared in her path, Emilia swerved to avoid hitting her. Instead, she drove straight into the wall. The car crumpled on impact with the stone. Her lung was punctured by a broken rib as the shattered steering column drove into her chest. Her last thought was how angry her husband would be when he saw the damage to his car.

In the morning, a passing farmer would stop his tractor to check on the crashed car that had half demolished his wall. He would find Emilia crushed and dead, her face pale with guilt, her eyes staring ahead into emptiness. Her husband Piotr would retrieve the wreckage and her packed bags from the back seat. He would never know why she had driven away from him and the children that evening, resolved to end their marriage without a word.

Manson's body cracked the windscreen and dented the bonnet of a Mercedes driven by a drunk businessman. He stopped at once, causing two other cars to swerve to avoid piling into his bumper. Once called, the police quickly sealed off the carriageway and diverted traffic. The driver was charged, and Manson was declared dead at the scene, his neck broken and his spine ripped and riven. His eyes were closed, as if he had braced himself for the impact before landing.

Although Manson and Emilia were both dead, their story did not end there.

It was once again the evening of the same day in May. The Prime Minister had resigned. Emilia had left her children and her husband and taken his car. Manson's last thread had unravelled, and he had settled on a course of action that would lead to oblivion. At least, that was what he wanted that night.

Having spotted the man holding onto the barrier at the side of the bridge, Emilia had braked hard. She nearly drove past, but something drew her eyes to the man in the twilight. Zipping up her hoodie, she left the car and ran over to him. Manson heard the vehicle come to a stop, and sensed the woman arrive beside him before she spoke.

'Hello?' Emilia said. 'Are you okay?'

Manson's knuckles whitened as his grip tightened on the rail. 'Yes thanks,' he replied.

'I mean, do you need some help? It doesn't seem safe.'

His laugh was hollow. 'Ha, well, life isn't safe.'

Overcome with a wave of realisation, Emilia withdrew. 'I knew you were going to say that,' she said, shocked.

'Sorry to be so predictable. Please leave me alone.'

'I can't. I… Don't you remember me?' The fear of what was to come was rising within her.

'No. Should I?' He looked at her, in her hoodie and jeans, her hair tied back in a scrunchie. 'You're not that memorable.'

'We've done this before. Or at least I've seen it before.

Please don't jump.'

She reached forward impulsively to grab his arm. He flinched, letting go of the handrail. The movement caused him to lose his footing. Manson clutched at the air desperately as he fell backwards towards the road and surging traffic below. His face was full of fear, having lost control of his last moments. This was not how he wanted it to happen. It wasn't raining yet. The sickening thud of Manson's body against the speeding vehicle below brought Emilia to her knees.

Dazed, she wandered back to the car. Her phone was dead. Thinking only to get away from the scene and report her involvement, she sped away. Moments later, the car swerved to avoid a woman walking along the grass verge. The car hit a wall and Emilia was dead.

It was once again the same evening. The sun was minutes away from setting. The air was cooling, with the promise of rain. Manson held onto the rail, contemplating suicide. Emilia stopped her car on her way across the bridge and approached the man who, somehow, she recognised.

'Hello?' Emilia said. 'Are you okay?'

Manson's knuckles whitened as his grip tightened on the rail. 'Yes thanks,' he replied.

'I mean, do you need some help? It doesn't seem safe.'

His laugh was hollow. 'Ha, well, life isn't safe.'

Overcome with a wave of realisation, Emilia withdrew. 'I knew you were going to say that,' she said, shocked.

This time, Manson ignored her. Together, in silence, they waited for the rain. When it came, he closed his eyes and spread his arms as if he were about to fly. He let his weight tip forward, and he fell to his death below on the bonnet of a speeding Mercedes. Emilia walked back to her husband's car, stunned and emotionless. Once she started the engine, she wept with the inevitability of what was to come and drove her car around the pedestrian into the wall.

Although Manson and Emilia were both dead, for them the evening began again. When they met again on the bridge, the words came unbidden.

'Hello?' Emilia said. 'Are you okay?'

Manson's knuckles whitened as his grip tightened on the rail. 'Yes thanks,' he replied.

'I mean, do you need some help? It doesn't seem safe.'

His laugh was hollow. 'Ha, well, life isn't safe.'

This time, her laughter was as hollow as his. 'Death isn't either.'

Manson looked at her. 'What do you mean?'

'Why don't you remember? You died. I drove away, but then somehow ended up back here. Then it happened again. And again.'

There was some sort of distant recognition in Manson's eyes, but he said, 'I've never met you before. Who are you?'

'My name's Emilia. I was driving here, not really knowing where I was going. I took my husband's car and left him and the children. I was going to send for them once I had found somewhere to stay. I suppose I wasn't thinking clearly. I was upset.'

'Well, we all have shit to deal with. Leave me with

mine.' The sun was setting now, and Manson looked down at the passing cars and lorries below.

'Your name is Manson. You feel that your life is hopeless...'

'Why did you leave your husband?' He cut in, the question overriding his own self-obsessed thoughts.

Emilia was not ready for the question. She paused. 'I don't know,' she said, finally, furrowing her brow as if trying to retrieve the memory.

'Tell me or I'll jump right now, this second.' Manson's arms tensed.

'Okay, okay. I think... I think I left him because he wasn't letting me be me. I left behind education and a potential career in Poland for what was meant to be a better life. But we are still poor, we have children, and I am a cleaner. Piotr works as a builder during the day and a guard on the door of a nightclub at the weekends. He leaves me at home with the children. I think he is probably having an affair, but I don't know. I never see him, and...'

'Sounds to me like he's working hard to support his family and you're ungrateful.' Manson was dismissive. He closed his eyes and raised his face to the sky, waiting for the rain to come.

'Manson? I thought you would understand.' She was affronted, confused. He ignored her. 'Manson? Please don't ignore me,' she insisted.

The first drops of rain fell on Manson's cheeks. His eyes closed, he faced the sky, smiling peacefully, embracing the feeling of water on his skin. Enraged by his beatific expression and hurting from his careless words, Emilia shoved him in between his shoulder blades with both hands. He lost his grip and, without resisting, fell to his death below.

Emilia screamed with the guilt and inevitability of what she had done. This time, she had killed him. Frantically, she ran back to the car. Her keys were no longer in her pocket. She must have dropped them when she pushed Manson. Oh God, she had pushed him. She scrambled around in the shadows trying to find the keys on the ground, but with no success. The car was locked and she had no way to drive it now. But she had to get away, so she began walking. She decided to walk against the flow of any traffic and make her way along the grass verge towards whatever lay at the end of the bridge. She could find a farm building or a cottage and ask for help. Nobody would need to know that she pushed him. It was meant to be a suicide anyway, and it certainly would have looked like that. She would be in the clear, yet she still needed to report the man jumping from the bridge in case she had been seen driving there.

The car roared up behind her. There were no headlights on, and the driver must have only seen her walking in the same direction at the very last moment. The car was on the wrong side of the road, so could not have avoided the low stone wall that outlined the farmer's field. As it ploughed into the wall, the front end of the car was destroyed. It looked like the driver was killed instantly. And, in that instant, Emilia, standing in the rain on the grass verge, recognised the car. It was her own, taken from her husband that very evening.

The evening began again, and again Emilia found herself standing on the side of the bridge talking to a man who was about to leap down to a busy road and certain death.

'Hello?' Emilia said. 'Are you okay?'

Manson gave no answer this time.

'I mean, do you need some help? It doesn't seem safe.'

His laugh was hollow. 'Not even death is safe,' he said. He paused, then added, 'It's like we're haunting each other.'

In that moment, Emilia remembered everything. 'No. I think we're haunting ourselves,' she said.

'I know,' he replied, and threw himself off the bridge.

On the twenty-fifth day of May 2019, a tornado tore through Oklahoma, injuring thousands of people, and a boat capsized on a lake in the Democratic Republic of Congo, drowning dozens. It was the sixty-seventh day of spring.

Manson's ex-girlfriend was called upon to identify his body. She wept when she saw him, and grieved for months. When Emilia's husband Piotr retrieved her belongings, he chose not to see his wife in death. He would never know why she left him that night. In grief, he gave up his life in Britain and took his children home to his mother in Poland.

Since then, many drivers passing along that lonely road on rainy nights have reported glimpsing a lone man on the bridge or a lone woman, seemingly distressed, walking towards a ruined low stone wall on the other side. The sightings are usually dismissed as yet another unsubstantiated ghost story. Anyone who is curious enough to investigate will easily uncover the unremarkable stories behind the two tragic, seemingly unrelated, deaths that happened on that May evening in 2019.

FATHER'S DAY

I f the jazz bar had been in, say, New Orleans sixty summers earlier, it would be filled with smoke, beat poets and women who swirled and shimmied. Instead, in a rainy June in 2019, the jazz bar was in an Edinburgh basement filled with the ambient buzz of mobile phones, frequented by students and women accompanying their enthusiast husbands. Where once there was whisky and cigarettes, now there was craft beer and social media apps.

When Miles and his parents arrived at The Jazz Basement that night, they were greeted on the door by a tattooed Russian in a padded coat. His manicured beard and black hair tied back in a ponytail marked him out as a doorman to not tangle with, but his gleaming smile from his many gold fillings was disarming. As they approached, Dmitri welcomed them with his opening patter.

'Good evening,' the Russian said. 'Welcome to The Jazz Basement. Is this your first time here?'

As usual, Miles's mother Patience took charge. A bustling, sturdy Jamaican woman, she was used to speaking up for her more reserved husband. His intellectual superior, she was quick to assess a situation and, ironically, had little patience for his hesitancy in starting conversations with strangers. To Patience, a stranger was just someone who hadn't yet bent to her will. She returned a smile to the Russian doorman.

'Yes, it is,' she replied. 'Our son Miles has organised this as a treat for his father here.' She gestured towards Abegunde, her husband. Although he hailed from Nigeria and Patience and he had met in London once they had both moved to England, Abegunde was always faintly embarrassed that his name sounded a little too African for British ears. He preferred to go by Abe, which is what Patience had quickly christened him when they first met. He had inherited his father's love for jazz and named his own son after Miles Davis. He felt that the name Miles had a little more internationality. Jazz knew no colour, though, other than that which it painted with the chaos of its harmonies and diversions.

'It is ten pounds entry tonight for Chris Watkins and his band playing the music of Chet Baker. It will be very good. It is always popular,' said Dmitri with his glinting smile.

'Yes, of course,' Patience replied. 'We need to make sure we have seating, though. My husband's back and my knees, you see. I know we don't look it, but we're in our fifties.' She returned the smile, not quite sarcastically.

'You could go downstairs and check if there is a table?' the doorman suggested.

Before he could finish, Patience breezed past him down the stairs into the basement. Within a couple of minutes, she re-emerged with thumbs raised. Everyone nodded their approval, and Miles paid the doorman. Dmitri stamped their hands with the inky brand of The

Jazz Basement. 'Just in case you want to come back in after going out,' he said.

'Do people still do that?' said Abe.

'Dad,' Miles nudged. 'Don't embarrass me now. Anyway, we'll be staying, won't we? This is your Father's Day present, after all.'

'Yes. Yes, it is. He's a good boy,' Abe said to Dmitri.

As Miles stepped through the door, Dmitri said, 'Wait one moment.'

'What is it? You want to see my ID? I've got my student badge somewhere. I'm twenty...'

'No, no. I wanted to ask you and your father a question. You seem like the type who would be interested. Most people are not. But I can tell real jazz enthusiasts.'

Abe paused on the top stair, grabbed by the mischief of interest. Below, Patience had claimed the table and waited. Abe could already hear her chatting to somebody down there. 'Well, it runs in the family. What's the question?' he asked.

Dmitri leaned into a whisper. 'Do you know about the ghost?'

Abe laughed, but he was genuinely intrigued. 'The ghost? In that basement?'

'Oh yes. It is our little secret. We do not put it on our website or in our advertising. But we do like to advise some customers, especially when it is their first time. You see, The Jazz Basement is in a very old building, and it is haunted sometimes.'

'Sometimes?'

Dmitri winked. 'Sometimes, they say, the ghost of a famous jazz musician pays a visit during the night, joins in on stage, but he can only be seen by a select few. Usually just young enthusiasts on their first visit, eh?' He winked again at Miles, smiling that metal-tinged smile.

Laughing it off, Miles and his father made their way down the stairs, passing sticky handrails and peeling posters of gigs long past with musicians long gone. Abe paused at a reproduction of a Louis Armstrong performance at the Ritz Cafe in New Orleans. 'The world has come a long way since the only way a black man could listen to Louis Armstrong and his band was to sit on the road outside the nightclub. And the first time he picked up a horn was at the Coloured Waif's Home for Boys.'

'Yeah, yeah, and if he hadn't started playing The Star-Spangled Banner after Pearl Harbour with decades of slavery behind him, we might not have got Hendrix playing it and setting fire to his gee-tar, eh, Dad?'

'You can take the piss if you like but we're here now. A couple of hours of some of the best music in history, and I reserve the right to be as boring about it as I like.'

'Not boring, Dad.'

They found their seats at a little round table at the back of the room. Patience was already sitting there, sharing a joke with a young woman, who was collecting empty glasses. 'See, in his time, Louis Armstrong would have been able to play places like this, but he wouldn't be allowed to sit at a table like this,' said the older man, taking a seat next to his wife. 'And he paved the way for musicians like your Grandpa Chinua, my father. He toured on the same bill as a few of the greats, although he was always in the background, never played with any of the big names.'

'Told you my husband would hold forth on his jazz pedigree,' Patience said, gesturing extravagantly with her immaculately manicured hands, orange nail varnish luminescent in the gloom of the bar.

Blushing, the bar girl gathered up the glasses and headed back to the bar. 'I'll be over there when you want anything,' she said. 'The guys tonight are playing Chet Baker.'

'My husband is obsessed with him, like his father was, even though Chet Baker was a white man who wouldn't have had any problem getting a table anywhere.'

'Well, I think it's fair to say that Chet Baker had plenty of other problems of his own. My name's Kathryn. Just ask for me over there when you're ready,' she finished, then swished into the shadows past the barstools.

Miles watched her go. She looked vaguely familiar. Maybe he had seen her around the university. Miles was in the second year of his degree at the Reid School of Music at Edinburgh. Unlike his namesake, Miles had no facility for the trumpet. He was a pianist, and a good one. He had his classical repertoire and could busk most things he heard on the radio by ear, so he found himself increasingly drawn to the challenge of jazz. It turned order into chaos, threw it around, and assembled it back again in a new order. He loved it, and it was a love passed on by his father and his father's father.

The basement was warm with the chatter and expectation of people who sat at small circular tables, illuminated from the centre by jars of light. A spangly backdrop decorated the slightly elevated stage where the band were setting up. Looking like a day trip of accountants and supply teachers in their shirts and chinos, the five-piece jammed away through a half-hearted soundcheck. Piano, drums, double bass, saxophone all had a burst. The trumpet player was curiously quiet, standing nervously over to one side, seemingly assembling his thoughts. A slender man with a stark jawline and hair that flopped over his glasses, Chris Watkins held his trumpet in the crook of his arm. Miles glanced at him, and thought how cool it was that a musician about to dip into the Chet Baker catalogue already looked the part before he even blew the first note.

At the bar, Miles caught Kathryn's eye. She wiped the counter, tucked away a couple of dirty glasses, and nodded acknowledgement. 'Drinks then?' she asked. She had wisps of hair that strayed through her fingers as she swept it all back into a ponytail. She was just a little bit older than him: not so old that it would seem indecent to ask her out; not so close in age that he could feel emboldened. Miles quickly dismissed the idea. Being with his parents on a night out would hardly help his chances anyway.

Miles selected a couple of bottled beers for himself and his father. 'Can I also have a coffee, please?' he added, feeling faintly ridiculous.

'Coming right up.' Clearly, ordering an Americano with milk on the side and a free biscuit wasn't all that ridiculous in The Jazz Basement. She set the coffee machine going, then popped open the beers. 'Your parents are fans of Chet Baker then?' she asked.

Miles hovered his phone over the machine to pay. It

bleeped, extracting money from his bank. 'Sort of. Dad is. Grandad was a session player, and toured with a few ensembles, so we sort of inherited it. Dad named me after Miles Davis, in fact. I'm planning to name my first child Lady GaGa.'

Kathryn indulged his joke with a chuckle. She laid out the coffee for him. The spoon tinkled on the edge of the saucer. 'Did Dmitri tell you about the ghost?'

'Yeah. I assumed he was joking. Is it a thing, then?'

'Apparently. Not seen it myself. Not for want of trying, either. I kind of got interested in that sort of thing a few months ago.'

'Yeah?'

'Long story. Haven't seen anything yet, though. But Edinburgh is supposedly very haunted indeed, so keep an eye out.' Another customer waved for Kathryn's attention, so she went over to the end of the bar to serve him. Miles took the drinks back to the table and settled down to watch the band. He clinked bottles with his father.

'Happy Father's Day, Dad,' he said.

'Well, it's not until Sunday, but I'll take that. Well done, my boy. This is a good place,' Abe replied, looking around the room. His wife smiled quietly to herself, winked at her son, and slurped her coffee. Satisfied that he had pleased his parents for once, Miles sipped his beer. 'Although,' he added, 'if they mar Chet Baker's memory, I won't be very charitable.'

'I'm sure they'll do him justice,' Patience reassured him, half-mocking. 'He can hardly complain. Even if he was still around, he'd be, what, ninety?'

'Something like that.'

Miles was excited by having some common conversational territory with his parents. It was a rarity these days. He enjoyed giving his father the opportunity to hold forth on his favourite subjects, even if he'd heard the stories dozens of times before. 'How did Chet Baker die anyway, Dad? Heroin overdose, wasn't it?'

Abe flashed with irritation. 'No. He was a junkie, true, but he loved jazz more than getting high, even towards the end. It wasn't the drugs that killed him.'

'No?'

Abe gave his son a gentle thump on the arm. 'No. He fell off a hotel balcony in Amsterdam.'

'Because he was on drugs?' Miles laughed.

'Well, maybe there was some heroin involved. Who knows?'

There was some warm whistling and cheering as the musicians took to the stage in the corner of the bar. Producing a comb from his pocket, Chris Watkins styled his hair after Chet Baker, slicked back as if he had walked out of the 1950s. But when he spoke, it was with a Glaswegian twinge, and he introduced the first number. After some shuffling, they opened with the piano of "Let's Get Lost", not a Baker original but a jazz standard that he made his own. Watkins' voice was a little too thin to replicate the smoothness of 1955, but his trumpet was good enough for Abe, who nodded along. Watkins introduced his piano player, who elicited polite applause from the audience as he did his best impression of Russ Freeman's playing on the original, and led Watkins into "Autumn Leaves", where he proved he could divert into real jazz territory alongside the drummer's gentle syncopation.

'Not bad,' Abe winked at his son. 'Of course,' he said, 'you know Baker barely wrote anything himself. This one was from some French film, originally, I think. He did most of his composing in the sixties after he came out of prison.'

'What was he in prison for?'

'That time it was drug charges in Italy, you'll be disappointed to hear.' Abe laughed. 'Get me another drink, son?'

Just as Miles got up to go, his mother patted his arm. 'Talking of drugs...' she began.

'No, Mum, I'm not on heroin. Or crack.'

'No, idiot. Your medicine.'

Miles had been experiencing low blood pressure after a bout of a particularly pernicious virus that had been doing the rounds, so his doctor had prescribed some medication, lots of fluids, and regular exercise. He felt he was doing all of that already, so had been cutting back on alcohol. Tonight, in fact, was the first time he'd had a drink in several weeks. He wasn't going to leave his Dad to drink alone.

'Don't fuss, Mum. I'm taking the pills. I'm okay. Really. It was just the after-effects of a virus. I'm not dying.' In truth, Miles had forgotten to take the medication that night, but one night wouldn't matter.

Patience scowled disapprovingly. 'Take things seriously,' she said. Playfully, Miles blew his mother a kiss and, despite herself, she laughed. She waved him on to the bar.

Miles returned to the bar just as the band segued into "How High the Moon". The bar was quiet, with most of the clientele sitting listening to the piano player going off into his own scale-strewn jazz world until Watkins reined him back in with the trumpet. Kathryn served up another round for Miles.

'Enjoying it?' she asked.

'Yeah. Love it, in fact,' Miles replied.

'A lot of jazz leaves me cold, but this is okay.'

'High praise.'

'So, did your Grandad play here?'

'I don't know. Dad didn't say he had, but there's a lot that Dad doesn't say. It was a long time ago.'

'Well, apparently this has been a jazz club for, like, forever, so maybe. You never know.'

'You never know.' Miles took the drinks back to the table, where his parents were sitting more closely together, Patience's head on Abe's shoulder, as they listened to the band.

'You two,' Miles joked, 'you should get a room.'

Abe laughed. Patience pretended to scowl. Miles sat down, silently congratulating himself on having parents that were at least a little less embarrassing than most people his age claimed theirs to be.

The audience applauded as Chris Watkins finished a breathless solo and announced that there would now be an interval. He and the rest of the band went straight to the bar. The lights stayed dim, and murmurs of appreciation and warm friendly conversation from the rest of the clientele filled the stuffy air. As Miles watched Kathryn serving the members of the band, chatting to them animatedly, his eyes lost focus as if he were suddenly very tired. He blinked hard.

'You alright, son?' His father's voice came in faintly through a miasma that dissipated as soon as it had enveloped him. Miles blinked again, aware of feeling slightly faint.

'I'm okay,' he said. 'I'll just go to the loo, splash some water on my face.'

He stood up, and swayed slightly. He steadied himself on the back of the chair and straightened his back. 'Honestly, I'm fine,' he said.

'Want me to come with you?' Abe asked, his brow furrowed in concern for his son.

'Nah, I can manage. I'll be back in a sec.'

As Miles swung through the door marked 'Gentlemen', he blinked at the sudden change in lighting. The striplight was harsh, stabbing his eyeballs. The bathroom was functional: clean and recently refurbished. Public toilets were never a joy to visit. In and out as quickly as possible, that was the way. All the cubicles were free, so Miles avoided the less private urinal. Having finished, he zipped up, flushed, then turned back to the sinks to wash his hands.

Miles must have turned too quickly, he thought, as he felt dizzy in that instant. Unsteadiness buzzed around his head and he swayed, having to steady himself against a cubicle's door frame. He squeezed his eyes tight and paused, breathing steadily. In. Out. In. Out.

When Miles opened his eyes, the light was different. The bathroom was not as he remembered it a minute or two earlier. The bathroom was all white tiles and freestanding sinks. The taps, rather than dribbling out a portion of water with a handwave, were the old type, one for hot, one for cold. The man at the nearest sink was just turning a tap off, having just washed his hands. He took a comb out of his back pocket and, appraising himself in the mirror, tended to his hair. He teased it into a sculpted smoothness and nodded approval to himself.

The man, in clean white t-shirt and high-waisted trousers, seemed familiar. For a moment, Miles assumed it was Chris Watkins, taking a toilet break before the second half of his performance. But no. It was unmistakable. Miles had seen enough photographs, and studied his father's records until he knew every word of every sleeve note, every image printed on paper and cardboard.

Miles was looking at Chet Baker, young and sleek, as he was in the nineteen-fifties. Before the drugs, before the sunken cheeks and lank hair, before the ignominious death falling from a balcony many years later. Chet turned away from his ablutions, and caught Miles staring at him.

Chet's voice was light, almost lugubrious, as if he was embarrassed to speak. 'Hey man, can I help you?' he said.

Miles blushed. He felt his cheeks prickle with his own embarrassment. 'You're Chet Baker?' he asked, finally.

'Uh… yes. You heard me play?'

'Yeah! I mean, yes, many times. Pleased to meet you,' Miles said, extending his hand in greeting.

Chet hesitated. His white hand hovered close to Miles' black skin, as if unsure. Sensing something, Miles was about to withdraw when Chet took his hand firmly. A handshake from Chet Baker, real and cool and solid. 'Your name, man?'

'Miles.'

'Miles. Nice. Like Miles Davis?'

'Yeah. In fact... How have you heard of him?'

Chet looked at Miles quizzically. 'Well, I'm not a hermit. He's my favourite trumpet player of the last couple of years. It's nineteen-fifty-five, not eighteen-fifty-five.' He gave Miles a smile that quickly faded. 'Anyway, bye now.'

Miles watched Chet disappear through the bathroom door out into the club. He stood for a moment, observing his own reflection in the mirror. He blinked, then looked again. Still the same. He followed Chet Baker out into the club.

The room was different from before. It was a much bigger auditorium, wider and longer. There were only a few tables over to the sides, and in the centre of the floor, couples were dancing. The clothes, the hair, the cigarette smoke - all of it was transported from nearly seventy years ago. Or had Miles been transported there?

The stage spread across the width of the club. A baby grand piano and drum kit took up most of the stage, but front and centre were two trumpet players and a saxophonist, jostling alongside a man with a double bass. The men were all in baggy suits, except for the jacketless Chet Baker, who walked shyly through the throng of dancers to take up his spot on the stage.

Through the gloom of smoky blue light, Miles blinked, squinting to see who was accompanying Chet Baker. It was impossible. They could never all be in the same place at the same time, surely. But here they were. Chet was the only white man onstage. At the piano, in a fedora, light suit and tie, the unmistakable figure of Thelonious Monk was picking out the opening phrase of "Pannonica". Although on record it was Ernie Henry and Sonny Rollins who would double up on saxophone a year later, here was the slender, serious John Coltrane swinging in. His warm saxophone decorated the song in a way that had never happened in reality. This could not be real, of course. Whatever was happening, it wasn't real. Miles decided he must be hallucinating, a result of not taking his medication on time. He had fainted and was dreaming. But it seemed so real. Art Blakey was taking it easy on the drums as Monk improvised up and down scales.

Shadows closed in, as if lights were being turned down on the crowd, until the dancers were simply shapes in the darkness. The musicians were spotlit. As Coltrane put his final flourish on Monk's song, Chet Baker stepped to the microphone. His cool, almost diffident, voice sang "Oh, You Crazy Moon". There was barely any time to pause when John Coltrane followed with the iconic opening to his own "Blue Train". On the recording that was yet to happen, Lee Morgan was on trumpet. Here, on this night, it was Chet Baker.

Miles edged his way around the darkened room, the people brushing past him indistinct blurs. At the bar, he looked for a familiar face, but of course there was no one. The barman, a slight man with a pencil moustache, passed Miles a shot of whisky without him asking. He nodded a thanks, and sniffed the drink. That was enough.

Not his thing, so he set it aside.

Chet's breathless voice cut through the hubbub. 'Thank you all. That was quite an experience. Now, we'd like to introduce a special guest on piano.'

The spotlight swivelled to illuminate Monk's replacement on the piano stool. Miles gasped. It was Grandpa Chinua, but under this light he could not have been aged more than twenty-five. Miles knew the face from family photo albums and his father's proud sharing of press cuttings and playbills from decades before. There was also the family resemblance. Everyone here was out of their own time, whilst playing in time with each other. Chet Baker. The other musicians. Miles himself. And his grandfather.

Chet introduced Chinua as 'Born in Nigeria, raised in Philadelphia, settled in London' to rapturous invisible applause. Chinua improvised a short solo, then started picking out delicate, hesitant chords as he introduced the next song.

'On this Father's Day, I'd like to dedicate this song to all the fathers far and wide, young and old, living or not. This is simply called "Abe". Hope you like it,' Chinua said. It was a gutsy ballad that spiralled and grew on the piano, until Coltrane burst in with a saxophone solo that took the melody line in his own direction. Chet took the line and his trumpet solo took it elsewhere again until the tune meandered back to Chinua at the piano, where he closed off with a quiet coda like raindrops on ice.

Miles stayed at the bar, as the dark shapes around him solidified into black corners. The music came to an end, and very soon all he could see, as if walking through a tunnel of light that parted the darkness, was his grandfather, young and smart in his suit and tie, coming towards him. Chinua drew on a cigarette and extended a hand to Miles. Miles took it, shaking hands with his grandfather as an equal in age, if not in status.

'Thanks for coming, Miles,' Chinua said.

'You know who I am?'

'Of course, man. My boy's boy. Couldn't be prouder of you. And Abe, of course. He got himself a woman who's more than a match for him, ain't he?' Chinua laughed, a huge belly laugh that belied his athletic shape. 'And your momma gave us you, Miles. Lookin' good there, my man!'

'Thanks, er... Grandad. How? I mean... are we dead?'

Chinua laughed again. 'Well, I know I am. As is everyone else here. And none of us look like we did when we died. You wouldn't have wanted to see that,' he chuckled. The laughter punctuated every utterance.

'So, you're...'

'A ghost? Woooooooo! Ain't nothin' more jazz than that, is there?'

'I'd never heard you play like that. You were amazing. I hope I can get to be half as good.'

'Oh, you will. Be half as good, that is!' He laughed once more, winking. 'Listen, Miles, you can tell your Dad that I finally got to play with all the greats. Except Miles Davis. He's in the other place. Maybe.'

Miles' mouth dropped open. Chinua winked and took a slug of whisky from Miles' forgotten glass. He waved casually to the barman to bring him another drink. 'I'm gonna stay here and have a drink or two with Baker, Coltrane and the others. We'll trade stories and shoot the breeze until it's all dark. You don't wanna be here when that happens, so why don't you go splash some water on your face? You remember where the Men's Room is?'

Miles nodded. 'Thank you, Grandpa,' he said.

Chinua raised his glass in farewell.

The harsh light in the bathroom took Miles by surprise. He immediately felt a spray of dizziness prickle his skin, and his knees buckled. He didn't feel himself hit the floor.

When Miles came round, he had been pulled to his feet and dragged into a chair. The faces of his father, mother and Kathryn-from-the-bar were looming over him. Too close. He winced, and they all pulled back, relaxing as he came to consciousness. 'What are you doing?' he said.

'You passed out in the toilets,' said Kathryn. 'Your Mum called me over when your Dad went in to find you. I'll go and get you a drink of water.' She whisked out of his sight.

The room was full, the audience chattering and enjoying their own business, oblivious to this family with the fainting son and fussing parents. Kathryn returned with a glass of water. 'Catch you later,' she said, and returned to the bar.

Patience scowled disapprovingly at her son. 'I told you to take your medicine,' she scolded.

'How long was I out?' asked Miles, sipping his water.

'About ten seconds,' said Abe. 'I heard a bump and thought it must be you, falling over. So, I dragged you out and here we are. You gave us a bit of a fright there, son. You look really pale. You look like you've seen a ghost.'

Miles laughed, a belly laugh that belied his less-than-athletic shape.

A couple of weeks later, after Patience and Abe had taken the train back home to London, leaving with Miles instructions to eat properly and take care of himself, he was heading home to his student bedsit after a late rehearsal, with a sheaf of musical notation tucked under his arm. He had just seen a few friends home to their shared accommodation in Edinburgh Old Town and stepped into a coffee shop on Cockburn Street for a takeaway flat white. Whilst he waited, Miles perused the tables idly. Sitting at a table in the window with a laptop and a large latte was Kathryn. She was dressed for a June evening, in a printed dress over a Ramones t-shirt, and heavy laced-up boots.

His coffee in hand, Miles stopped at her table on the way over. It took her a moment to recognise him out of context of the gloomy bar, but her reaction was not unwelcoming. 'Miles! How are you?' she asked.

'Oh, I'm fine. Low blood pressure. Took my tablets. I'm okay now. What are you up to?' he said, nodding towards her laptop and open notebook. A little direct, he thought, but why not?

'Oh, this and that. Getting ready for my research project. I'm not just a barmaid, y'know,' she smiled.

'Obviously! Listen, you know we were talking about ghosts?'

'Yes?' She was wary but interested now. They sat together and sipped their coffees, and Miles told her of hallucinations, jazz musicians, a grandfather and a handshake.

'Do you believe me?' Miles asked, toying with his cup. He had let his coffee grow cold.

'Does it matter? I've seen some weird stuff myself. Anyway, it's time I was on my way,' she replied, as she started packing up her belongings into her backpack.

'Cool.' Miles took a deep breath. 'I don't suppose you…'

Before he could finish, she threw him a smile that felt like music. 'There's a ghost of chance, I suppose,' she said.

EUTIERRIA

Parking the car is easy. The crunch of gravel under the tyres alerts the dog to where we are. She starts whimpering, stands up on the back seat, pacing from side to side. If she could open the door herself, she would. Unlike the kids, who would sit there and demand that the chauffeur open the door for them no matter what. I climb out, gathering up my phone, keys, and big old stick with a groove in it for my thumb. I make sure nothing is showing on the seats or footwells that would make anyone want to break into the car. I flatter myself that my Porcupine Tree CDs would be of any interest to passing would-be thieves and tuck them out of sight. I walk around to the door on the other side to let the dog out. She lets out a little excited bark as I take just that little too long to pull the handle. When I do open the door, she bounces down and immediately heads over to the undergrowth for an investigatory sniff.

'Wait,' I say, so she waits. I clip her lead on to her harness, lock the car, and we're off.

It's still early. The woods are cool, especially today, when the air is still, and the sun has yet to burn through the clouds. The dog loves it here, in as much as you can say a dog loves anything. I entertain the idea that she has complex emotions, but in truth she is driven by smells, of which there are plenty here. If I left her here, abandoned, I wonder how long it would take before she exhausted the novelty of new smells and squirrels to chase and started pining for home. Dogs adapt, but I suppose she's too domesticated to go back to the wild and live in the woods. I wonder if I could do it.

We take the path off the layby. The dog trots ahead, snuffling the hedgerows. She selects a spot to take a piss and crouches down. She must have been hanging on since before we left the house, because it takes a minute to finish. Panting a smile, she's pleased with her achievement. I congratulate her with a scratch behind the ears and an enthusiastic tummy rub, and encourage her to run on, which she does, checking every so often that I'm following. My knee is hurting today, so the stick helps. It's a useful height so I can lean my weight on it without falling over or worrying my fat bulk will cause it to snap. I'm not that fat I suppose, just averagely overweight for my age, and not as fit as I should be, what with the high blood pressure and everything else.

The trees are a contorted canopy above us, trunks split and twisted back around each other. It's a reassuring tangle, like fingers crossed over each other, hands forming an arch the way you do when you're making out that you're thinking really hard. These arboreal bouncers stand guard around the clearing, eyeing me up and down, assessing whether I'm permitted entry, whether my membership has expired, whether I look like the right clientele. They wave the dog through regardless, so I suppose I get to go in as her guest.

It's almost enough to make you forget your

worries. The dog takes off after a movement in the bushes. Whether it's a real squirrel or an imagined one doesn't matter; she's off. As she crashes around, I look up at the canopy of trees, nothing swaying as there is no breeze. The nearest tree is like a set of conjoined triplets. A long time ago, either the trunk got split by lightning from a great and magic axe wielded by a Norse god, or three trees liked each other very much and decided to live entwined for the rest of their lives. Whichever it is, it starts as one tree but then, about a foot off the ground, three separate trunks have grown upwards and upwards. The upper branches intertwine in places, but the lower ones have been lopped neatly: someone has been round with a saw. Three trees bound together for all eternity.

I used to think that would be me: bound to another soul until I end up rooted in the ground myself. I was proved wrong. Ten years ago today, I lost Carol. Marriage wasn't forever, even though we'd both promised. You can make a promise, you can even mean it, but in the end it doesn't make any difference if there are other plans in place. The last couple of years with my second wife Clare have been hard. Her bloody kids. That's another reason why I got this dog, so I've got an excuse to get out of the house. It's just me and the dog, with the air and the quiet, and every now and then, we come to these woods.

The dog bounds back towards me, with no prize from her miniature hunting expedition other than a lolling tongue and a wagging tail. From this clearing, there are three paths: one continues the well-worn path we were on, taking a circuitous route around the wood back to the road; another does similar but heads the other way; the third is the proverbial less-trodden, criss-crossed with fallen boughs and dips that flood when it rains. You can guess which one the dog takes. I let her choose. I've got legs. I can climb over things and muddy boots can be cleaned. Besides, it might take a bit longer and then I won't feel the need to rush back to the house and Clare's kids with their phones, consoles, busy screens, and blank stares.

I've lost sight of the dog. She's tramping through brambles, diving after wriggling and rustling things on the forest floor like an electric strimmer, so I can hear her. I can't follow the sound exactly, as I have to step over a fallen tree to get to her. The tree's bark has yet to be ravaged by moss and insects, so its fall must be relatively recent. I'm not going to investigate its roots, but two thirds of the way along its length, it bisects like a pair of legs. Its crotch mysterious and blank, each leg has grown to escape the other one. The lower one has succumbed to weight and is reclining on the ground. The upper one seemingly already had a life of its own before it fell, branching off again. Each branch is now buried in the green masses of another tree, one that I suspect is singularly unimpressed with having to break the fall.

I wonder how much trees are even aware of each other. I know there are theories, both outlandish and scientific, but it would be good to know whether they have some sort of telepathy or whether they live their long lives languishing inside themselves like we do. I don't know what I'd do with that information, mind. It would be terrifying to know what trees are thinking when we climb them, cut them down or, worse, when my dog pisses against them.

The dog's head pops up and I can see where she is. I sit on the fallen trunk, then swivel around, swinging my legs over as best I can. I'm too old to get over any other way. There was a time, of course, when I'd take a running jump and clear it easily but I'm certainly not fifteen anymore. She sees me and comes bounding back for some approbation, which of course she gets. I rub her head, fuss her behind the ears, and she's happy. She's looking for a dog treat. She knows they're in my pocket but I'm saving them for when I need to bribe her to get back into the car later. I wave her on and she trots off again, with me following along the brambly path. I could almost do this all day.

The path through the woods is cool. The morning sun is starting to come through, but we're still shielded, in our leafy cocoon. It's such a relief to be out and about without sweltering after five minutes. Last week's heatwave was too much, the hottest it's been for years. I think they said on the news that one day last week was the hottest on record. We kept the curtains drawn and the windows closed. With Clare working from home, I had to come clean and tell her about my job, that I'd taken garden leave. It was mutual, I said. I'll get another job no problem, I said. She just looked at me and didn't need to say anything to make me feel like a selfish piece of shit. But, today, that's the least of my worries. Bruce Springsteen's *Lonesome Day* runs through my head, and I hum the chorus as I hack at the tangled vegetation at my feet with my stick.

I suppose I am feeling lonesome, if that's the right word. There just doesn't seem to be much to show for a lived life after all this time. I've stacked up a few experiences, sure, but have I achieved all that much in my fifty years? I had a first marriage that didn't end in a way anybody could have predicted, a few years inside myself and working a job that is making me obsolete, and now a second marriage that is waning in a way everybody should have predicted. The dog and I get on fine, but dogs are pretty resilient. They might get attached to a person, but take that away and they'll just transfer their affections to whoever's feeding them every day.

I wonder if the dog would miss me at all if I just turned around and left her here. I wonder whether I'd be missed at home if I drove off and never came back. Sometimes, it feels like the right course of action, the thing to do, but I don't know where I'd end up, probably driving up and down the motorway in an endless, aimless loop. Besides, I wouldn't be here to see the dog taking a shit behind a log like she is now. I take a look but it's too messy to pick up easily, so I kick some forest floor detritus over it to hide it, like a little tomb, a tiny barrow for an ancient chieftain made of dogshit. A clump of mushrooms, dark-helmeted and shiny, stand guard like riot policemen over the little memorial to my dog's defecation. She pads off again and I follow, steadying myself with the stick. My knee is just about managing.

When I was young, aged about ten or eleven, there were some woods near our house. They backed out onto some army barracks, and there was a tramp who lived in the woods. He had built himself a bivouac that he augmented, over the years, with a proper bed, bolstered roof, and even a little library. He was set up on the edge of a little clearing and had a fire on the go almost constantly so he could boil water for his tea, cook his food, and have a little warmth. My friends and I would pedal up there on our Raleigh Chopper bikes and visit him. A couple of them took the piss and only came the once, but my mate Greg and I went a bit more often. I don't even remember his name now, but the tramp must have been around my age now, and the story was that he'd been discharged from the army but had nowhere to go, so he camped down in the woods. The army knew he was there, the local police knew he was there, most of the kids in the area knew he was there, but no one much cared. He did no harm, we thought. We'd sit and make toast on his fire and listen to him tell rambling, semi-coherent stories, all the time lying on his mattress in his makeshift tent whilst we did wheelies around the campfire.

I don't live around there anymore. When I first moved down this way, it was just weeks after Carol's funeral. I sold the house as quickly as I could. We didn't have kids, so it was easy, straightforward. My buyer was a first-timer and I wasn't buying anything else, so it was done quickly. I came down here, rented a flat and got a job that paid the bills. I'd lost all ambition when she died. That was when I got my first dog and discovered the woods. He and I would come here at least once a week, even when it was chucking it down with rain or the snow painted the trees and plastered the ground. He lasted a good few years, even though he was a good age when I got him from the rescue centre. When I had to send him off,

I sat in the vet's waiting room for an hour and wept more than I had when Carol died. I eventually got replacements for both.

I had been on my own for about three years before Clare and I met and, to be honest, I was a steaming mess. We wandered into each other's lives and, before we knew it, we were comfortable and set. I never really thought about it until she started making marriage noises. We'd both been married before: she a divorcee with two children as part of the package; me a widower with a void that was sucking in gravity; but it seemed to be the thing to do. I proposed more because it seemed to be what I was supposed to do rather than something I really wanted. But whatever. We got a bigger place together, pooled our resources and, pretty soon, we were the unit you're supposed to be, with two kids and a dog. It seemed to be the thing to do, especially as I didn't have the whole package the first time around. The first time, we'd just run out of time, although we had tried. We tried.

To think I used to be something of a teenage athlete. I'd run cross-country for the school, ploughing on and on, steady and sure, always finishing, always seeing it through, but never quite winning. I was always second or third: respectable performances but never the ones that anyone remembers. But that was when I met Carol.

She was more or less the same age as me and stood at the side of the track with her friends, hanging about after school when the others had gone home. They weren't there for my benefit, though. Carol was the gooseberry for her friend Gemma, a diminutive, round-faced girl who had eyes for one of the other lads. I don't even remember who he was now, but it was the eighties so he had a mullet, an earring and wore his blazer sleeves halfway up his arms as if he was in *Miami Vice*. No mullet for me – my mother cut my hair, and you could tell. Carol and I hit it off though, bonding over Tears for Fears and Joy Division. We were teenagers. Music was important. Still is. I don't think the object of Gemma's affections even owned any records, but they had a snog one evening at the end of the playing fields with us all watching, laughing. We all went to get some chips on the way home and Carol decided she and I were going out together. She claimed me and that was that.

To this day, I have no idea what Carol saw in me, especially at that age. We were always so different from each other: me clumsy, she composed; me tactless, she thoughtful; me with wandering hands, she with tightly crossed legs.

The woods remind me of the time when all that changed. Those other woods of my childhood, where the old army fella read his books and warmed his feet by the fire, were so long ago in another time, another world. The last time I went there, the ex-soldier was long gone: we had forgotten about him when we went to secondary school and, by the time Greg and I decided to pay him a return visit, his tent was damp and empty, the books long overtaken by mould and soaked by rain, the last of his possessions trodden into the dirt. We never knew when he had died, and we never would. I looked for any evidence of the old man himself, but there was nothing. It was as if he'd soaked into the ground with the rain.

I imagined him there, just below the surface, sleeping under the grass.

The dog is panting. She lies down with a stick, so I sit on a fallen trunk, mossy and comfortable. I look around. The path seems suddenly unfamiliar; I'm not sure which way we came, and the clearing we're in is denser than I remember. A breeze whispers through the upper branches, but it doesn't stir the air. I wonder if I've imagined it.

The dog looks up at me. 'Shall we go home, girl?' I say. She gets my meaning and stands up. 'Come on then,' I say, and head back in the direction that I think we came from.

The path we take is overgrown, less well-trodden than I remember. We've clearly gone the wrong way, but the woods aren't that big, I reason. I'm sure we'll loop around. It's not like we're in a rainforest with predators around every corner. The path disappears now, so overgrown that I have to kick my way through. It's like I'm just standing in a bush, thorns scratching and catching on my clothes. Give them a couple of months and they'll be sporting blackberries, but right now they're just snagging and dragging. Something skitters and the dog's ears prick up. She dives into the undergrowth and thrashes about vainly. When she emerges, she is on the other side of the mass of brambles. I stamp it down so I can step over to join her.

Another path crosses where we are, seemingly separating two forests. But that can't be. I've been here dozens of times and I've never seen this area. I must be more tired than I thought I was. Last night took more out of me than I had realised. The dog trots over there, investigating new smells, so I follow. It's suddenly cooler somehow, the smell of the trees in the air.

Leaves are on the ground, brown, beige, and brittle. Some have been trodden almost into mulch, soggy with old rainfall. I step around a puddle, slick and muddy. The dog is sniffing the air, and I can sense it too. That word. Petrichor. The smell of the earth after rain. Really, it's not all that unusual for isolated spots to have had rain when the rest of the area is dry. It usually means an isolated cloud is on the move, or I'm walking into or out of it. That's what I tell myself, anyway. It certainly feels unusual enough.

Oak trees rise up around us, the forest floor thick with the crust of fallen autumnal leaves. I really am losing my grip more than usual. I could have sworn it was summer when I left home this morning. Sometimes, the way I remember things doesn't seem to be the way that some other people remember it, so maybe this is another example of me starting to lose it. That's why I like the woods so much: it gives me a respite from distractions, from the worry of not getting it right and the judgement of people.

The oak leaves, interspersed with the shed material of other trees and the plant corpses of the forest floor, form a vast unsolved jigsaw, spreading out beneath the branches. A few feet from the base of the largest oak is something man-made. A makeshift crucifix, made from two twigs no more than an inch each in diameter, tied together with an old shoelace and some blue twine, stands in the ground. Placed at its base, wrapped in a thin plastic bag, the type used to secure leftovers for the freezer, is a framed photograph.

The frame is silver-coated plastic, barely visible through the misty milkiness of the bag. Mould and condensation spots further obscure the details, but a photograph is in the frame. It seems to be an image of a middle-aged couple, the woman with pale skin and shoulders in a dress, and the man slightly taller in a dark suit with something on the lapel. His face is as faint and misty as hers, indistinct through the plastic and condensation.

I bend to pick it up, ignoring the pang in my knee. I hesitate with my hand just an inch away from the wet plastic. I get the feeling suddenly that I shouldn't disturb it, like it's an actual grave or sacred burial site. But it's just a photo wrapped in a sandwich bag. A photo wrapped in a sandwich bag amongst damp autumn leaves in a forest. A forest that was fresh with summer sun just a few minutes ago.

Carol and I got married earlier than anybody should. We were so young, barely in our twenties, eyes wide open welcoming the life to come that we thought we would experience together. We had no idea really. Registry office, nice reception paid for by her parents, honeymoon somewhere hot with cheap booze and a communal swimming pool, home to a rented flat with a single storage heater. Not before too long, we'd graduated to our first house: a starter box with two bedrooms and nowhere to store the vacuum cleaner. I'd often trip over it on the landing on my way to have a piss in the middle of the night. We meandered along for a few years: I'd trained as a teacher so always had work. Carol lurched from office job to office job, far cleverer and more patient than me, but unlucky with finding something that would stick.

One afternoon, Carol was waiting for me when I got home from work with a splitting plastic bag full of books to mark. She handed me a cup of tea and a teary smile that could only mean one thing. 'I'm pregnant,' she said, simply. I said, 'Holy shit,' but smiled as well. I might even have started crying. We were older than many first-time parents, but younger than we'd planned to be. But we embraced it and she threw herself into choosing prams and cots and all the other paraphernalia that Mothercare had to offer.

After she lost the baby, she was never the same again. Both of us seemed to have left something of ourselves behind in that hospital that night. When she eventually fell ill a few years later, Carol told me with a mixture of equanimity and relief, as if it was what she had expected. The last time we spoke, in a brightly lit room with machines and white sheets, she talked of walking in the woods. In her drugged state, full of pills and comfort, she walked the same path as I did this morning, a child's hand in hers: a child who skipped ahead down the lane, beckoning her to follow.

Today, on the anniversary of Carol's death, I sit on the forest floor, staring at a damp photograph in a plastic bag. I pierce the plastic with my thumbnail and wipe the glass with the back of my hand. Mould has long obscured their features, but the man looks a little overweight, grimacing at the camera as if it's painful for him to stand. The woman – probably his wife – looks a lot like Carol, but I can't see clearly enough. I wipe my eyes and look again. I drop the photo frame in the dirt.

I lie back on the leaves, which feel somehow warm and dry again. The dog snuffles next to me, then her ears suddenly prick up. I hear another dog's bark somewhere along the track: it seems strangely familiar. She looks at me, wagging, as if asking permission to investigate. I wave her off and she bounds through the leaves, barking to the other dog.

Above me is a sky of branches, a net of foliage through which I can see glimpses of sun and cloud. As I close my eyes and my fingers dig into the soil, I forget what brought me here. I breathe the earth, I taste the air, and I take root. I see the whispers of memory in the wood. I hear the blaze of morning in the sun. The forest is with me as my heart slows.

BANK HOLIDAY

L ondon's deepest underground train station is North End. Located near the summit of a hill, the station was sunk to sixty-eight metres below ground, the deepest point on the entire Tube network. North End, though, is a ghost station. It was never completed and never opened. The deepest station that was actually operating in August 2019 was Hampstead, adjacent south-east to North End on the Northern Line. Hampstead boasted the deepest lift shafts, and it could be used as a way to access the abandoned tunnels of North End. Most passengers would never know of its existence, though. For them, the next stop after Hampstead was Golders Green.

In August 2019, Boris Johnson became Prime Minister and pledged billions of pounds to fund his 'No-Deal Brexit', whilst the country sweltered under a hot summer. July had seen a record thirty-eight Celsius in Cambridge in July, and August Bank Holiday Monday reached thirty-three degrees in London. Most people were able to enjoy the heat and sunshine, but unfortunately for Ricky Mover, he had to work.

Ricky was a telephone and communications engineer. It sounded more important than it was, as for him it meant spending his days in inhospitable places trying to fix old systems and rewire dangerous equipment. If it could be patched up rather than replaced, Ricky was sent in to deal with it. This is why he found himself getting ready to descend the hundred and ninety-seven steps down to the partially completed platforms of North End tube station on the hottest August UK bank holiday since records began.

Work began on building North End in 1903, but stopped when it was decided that the cancellation of a proposed housing development meant that there wouldn't be enough demand. Still, for three years, earth was tunnelled out, lift shafts were sunk, and platforms half formed before it ground to a halt in 1906. No buildings on the surface existed to mark out the presence of this forgotten vault of abandoned construction. Services on the Northern Line began in 1907, and trains thundered through the unfinished station, never stopping at North End. The soul of the station was left bereft, waiting for people who would never come.

Some people believe that places have a life of sorts, and when a place is left to die, it becomes a ghost, a phantom place, an aching absence with only the rats and shadows for company. Spirits of those lost and gone are drawn to those locations; people and places yearning for hope.

After World War Two, so many underground spaces in London were investigated as possible control rooms for civil defence, maintaining the floodgates for the Thames river, keeping essential services running in the event of nuclear war. Optimistically, a low building was constructed on the surface with an entrance leading to a deep shaft containing a spiral staircase and a one-man lift. Records have failed to show the exact reason why work stopped again in 1955. Perhaps the authorities realised the futility of developing such shelters in the face of a nuclear attack that would no doubt wipe out the entire population within seconds. Or perhaps there was another reason.

Quietly, and without fanfare, however, work continued on the floodgate control room, which was completed in 1956 and kept going until 1984. During that time, North End had a human presence, however intermittent, but engineers responded with dread when seeing North End assigned to their work rota. Rumour and urban legend grew once the control room became obsolete, replaced by the Thames Barrier. The men in charge were finally relieved to be able to lock the doors for what many hoped was the final time.

Abandoned again, North End's staircase languished in silence, each right-angle turning an insane approximation of a spiral, screwing down into the earth. Grey dust and mould settled into every surface, coating the rails, the brickwork, the steps down to tunnels that echoed with voiceless waiting. In 1997, two teenagers high on pills broke in, planning to graffiti the walls. They left in a hurry. When a passing patrol car happened upon them, pale and vomiting on the pavement, they would only say that they heard voices. Voices that whispered in languages that they couldn't understand, drifting up the stairwell. Today, the stairs are brightly lit with electric light so that the thirty-metre spiral could be used as an arduous emergency exit from Hampstead. Any evacuees would have to trek for eight hundred metres down the line first, of course.

Now, in August 2019, Ricky stood at the top of the staircase, looking down. In his orange overall boiler suit and hardhat, Ricky was already sweating. He was not enthralled by the prospect of heaving his weight down a staircase that was thirty metres straight down and God knows how long after all the angular turns. The air was stale and dry with dust. Two other men were with him, with their toolboxes and equipment that they now laid at his feet. Rahim was Ricky's supervisor, and Nigel was boss over them both, with responsibility for the day's work schedule.

'Right then,' said Nigel, bluff and business-like. 'There's a bunch of equipment to take down with you. Nothing too heavy, but your usual kit and you'll need to take some readings. But first, there's a fault on the lower landing telephone. If you can check that first, that would be good.' Nigel broke off to answer his phone. A question about shift patterns kept him occupied for a few minutes.

Ricky glanced at Rahim. 'Why aren't you going down instead of me?' he asked.

Rahim looked uncomfortable. 'Because I am checking the lines at this end,' he replied.

'I could do that. I've been on the team longer than you. You should go down.'

'This is what Nigel has asked us to do.'

'Bloody preferential treatment,' Ricky muttered, as he hoisted a bag onto his shoulder.

'Come again?' It was Nigel, coming off his call and

hearing the end of the conversation.

Ricky flashed his eyes at him, trying to communicate something he was reluctant to say. Nigel wasn't having any of it, and casually took off his glasses to wipe them with a handkerchief he kept in his pocket. Making a show of ignoring Ricky's gaze, he continued with, 'Is there a problem?'

Ricky lowered his voice, and turned his back to Rahim. He was trying to adopt a conspiratorial tone with Nigel. 'Look, you know what they're like. They come over in their boats, take all the benefits they can, then muscle in on our jobs. Come on, Nige, play the game, eh?'

Rahim busied himself with reviewing the paperwork as Nigel leaned in to reply to Ricky. As far as Nigel was concerned, Rahim had proved his mettle time and again since they took him on, hence the promotion. He had come from Syria with a degree in engineering, after all. 'Just do the job,' he said.

'Well, I'm not going down all those stairs - look at it!' Ricky exclaimed, pointing angrily at the bottomless view down through the staircase.

'You could go in the lift?' Rahim suggested.

'The vertical coffin?' Nigel laughed. 'I was going to suggest that anyway.'

'Oh, for fuck's sake,' Ricky replied, knowing he was defeated.

'Why is it called the vertical coffin?' Rahim asked.

'Because someone died in it,' Ricky sighed.

'No, they didn't. That's an urban myth. It's just a joke name - it's fitted for one person. That's the only reason. I think so, anyway,' said Nigel. Despite his efforts to give an air of authority, he couldn't help but chuckle at Ricky's annoyance. 'Right,' he continued, 'Rahim - I need you to go and check the control board. Ricky - just go down in the bloody lift. Deal with the fault, and then you can go down to the tunnel. I'll just go out for a quick vape, then I'll be right back up here. Clear?'

Ricky grumbled, but he took the two bags of tools to the lift anyway. Nigel was a bit older than him and could clearly handle himself in a fight if he had to, so Ricky would only push his luck so far. Rahim, though. If he could pin the blame on him for something, that would go a long way. Them. Taking jobs from British people. Getting in the way of his promotion. Rahim was one of them.

The lift door closed stiffly. Ricky secured it, made sure it clicked into place, then looked for the correct button to press. A single buzzing strip light in the roof of the lift illuminated the panel on the side of the lift. There was just enough room for Ricky to turn around, but it was definitely a one-person capsule. There were two buttons on the panel. One was an arrow pointing upwards for 'up'. The other was an arrow pointing downwards for 'down'. Ricky pressed the 'down' button, and the mechanism creaked into life.

Grinding gears inched the lift slowly downwards. It juddered twice, then something mechanical groaned as if it were reaching the end of its reach. With a jolt, the lift stopped. Ricky waited a moment for it to heave again. There was a distant clang and clatter several flights down, as if something small and metallic had fallen against something big and hollow. The lift hung, as if holding its breath.

Ricky swore, and pressed the 'down' button repeatedly. Nothing happened. He pressed the 'up' down again and again, each time waiting for a response that never came. Looking around for the alarm call button, Ricky began to panic. There was no alarm button. There was no way to alert anyone or summon help. He couldn't have gone very deep into the shaft, so maybe Rahim would be able to hear him if he shouted.

'Rahim!' he called. He waited a few seconds, then he called 'Rahim!' again. And again. Ricky soon escalated to 'Nigel!' a few times, then 'Help!' until he was hoarse.

'Shit,' Ricky said to himself. 'No one can hear me.'

The door handle was immovable; not only securely shut but impossible to budge even a millimetre. Ricky banged with the heel of his palm, then the side of his fist, then kicked with his boot against the door, the walls, the floor. Anything that would make a sound was worth a try. He continued until breathing became an effort and his limbs ached.

'Right. Don't panic. Listen. Maybe someone's coming,' he said. He felt faintly ridiculous talking to himself, but it seemed to help for a moment, at least. He held his breath to listen in the silence. Nothing.

Ricky glanced at his watch. Half an hour must have passed. If he just waited a bit longer, Nigel would have noticed that he hadn't reported back with the fault, and soon found out where he was. Unless he had left Rahim in charge. A sudden prickly realisation filled Ricky. He had given Rahim plenty of reasons to want to get back at him. Stuck in this lift, he was vulnerable. And it was his own fault.

'Rahim!' he called. 'It's not funny, mate! Let me out!'

Nothing.

'Rahim! For fuck's sake! Rahim!'

No reply. Ricky's voice bounced around the lift, a tiny metal box that carried no sound beyond its walls. Exhausted, Ricky collapsed against the shiny, scuffed metal that surrounded him. He caught sight of his own reflection, blurred and distorted slightly on the tarnished surface. He could see how sweaty and pale he was becoming. He sank to the floor, his knees under his chin with no room to extend his legs.

Above him, the strip light buzzed and crackled. Abruptly, something inside the light popped. Instant darkness fell. Ricky swore again. He felt around vainly for some sort of light switch, until it occurred to him that there would be a torch in his tool bag. Blindly, he grabbed the bag. Finding it, he soon located the ridged cylinder and his thumb pressed the button. The torch flickered into life, its beam a shaft of relief. Using the torch, Ricky finally ascertained that there were no other buttons to press, no hidden compartments, no way to rewire anything or find a manual release for the door.

To save the battery, he clicked off the torch. The darkness was solid, unrelenting. No ambient light meant there was no way to even see his hands. Still, Ricky closed his eyes, trying to calm himself. The only sounds he could hear were his own breathing and the thump of his heart. The latter was more of a vibration really, and he felt as if his heart were about to punch its way out of his chest.

If he just kept his eyes closed for a minute, let it subside, then he could start again making a noise. By then, Rahim might have given in or Nigel would have noticed.

Ricky must have fallen asleep, because when he next opened his eyes, he had the feeling of time having passed and he felt stiff, as if he had been in the same position for a period of time. Pins and needles prickled his legs, so he forced himself to his feet, which he stamped on the floor to get the sensation back. The next few minutes of banging and shouting were no more effective than the first, but more exhausting. It was growing warmer in there. It had been cool to begin with, a welcome relief from the temperature in the street, but now the discomfort was growing.

'What the hell am I going to do?' Ricky lamented to himself.

In the absence of light and sound, he felt a pressure in the air, as if something had moved in to fill a space. Something facing him. Something he could not see. He clicked the button on the torch. The beam flashed once, and in that half second, he saw a shape smeared against the stifling air: the suggestion of a face, eyes black and empty, mouth wide open in a silent scream.

'Fuck!' He dropped the torch. When he found it, groping in a panic, and turned it on again, the only face he could see was his own, reflecting back from the steel wall. In frustration, he banged and kicked and shouted again, to no avail.

Sitting on the floor, with his forehead pressed against his knees, he closed his eyes.

Ricky's awareness drifted, until he was awoken by the gentle lapping of water against his fingers. He opened his eyes to chaos: the splutter of a motor and the shouting of people. He was aboard a rigid-hulled inflatable dinghy, sitting on the edge, shoulder to shoulder with others. The boat was crammed: twenty people on a vessel made for eight at the most. Half were wearing orange life vests; half were soaking wet in hoodies and jeans - the only clothes that they owned. A girl, possibly Syrian like Rahim, maybe about ten years old, clutched tightly to a backpack on her lap. The arm of a cuddly toy stuck out from a gap in the zipper. Her father, his face dark with desperation, clutched even more tightly to her arm, steadying her each time the boat bounced over a wave.

'What the hell is this?' Ricky exclaimed.

A hooded, bearded man with a hefty life jacket and a French accent, was yelling orders to a group of passengers, including the girl with the backpack. When they stared back in panic, he switched to Arabic. Somehow, Ricky understood, although he knew he had no comprehension of the language before that moment. A spark of self-loathing inside him was quickly extinguished when he saw the man produce a pistol from his pocket.

The man waved his gun in the direction of the girl with the backpack. He was ordering her to throw it overboard. Water was already splashing in over the sides. Crying, calling for her mother, she held onto it all the more tightly, until her father wrested it from her grasp. Screaming, she reached for it as he dropped it over the side into the sea. As the girl tried to stand up, reaching to retrieve it, the boat became unbalanced. People panicked, moving to steady themselves as another wave threw the stern up into the air momentarily.

The boat fell back, the jolt pushing the girl off her feet. Losing her balance, she tumbled over the side. Screaming, her father desperately clutched for the strap of her life jacket. It slipped from his grasp. He appealed for help. The other passengers looked away, to themselves or their own loved ones, as the man with the gun shouted warnings.

Ricky looked down at his own helpless hands. He looked up. The father was diving after his daughter. With no life jacket, he was quickly engulfed and sank from sight. The girl's backpack had floated further away, and she struggled to stay afloat in the turbulent water.

Ricky had one thought only. 'I can swim,' he said. 'Who's with me?' he appealed to the boat. Nobody met his gaze.

The man with the gun screamed at Ricky, 'Get down!'

'Fuck you,' said Ricky, and dived into the water.

Vainly, Ricky swam around the bow of the boat towards the girl. Every stroke towards her seemed to send him further away. Caught in a current, he fought and fought, his arms and legs propelling him as best he could through the water. A wave swamped the girl. She choked on sea water, then she was gone.

'No!' Ricky's voice tore across the water as the distance between him, the drowned girl and the boat increased.

He gulped, trying to breathe, as water enclosed over him. His lungs filled with the sea, and warm darkness banished the cold.

When Ricky opened his eyes again, he was in the lift, smelling of metal and his own sweat. He swore quietly to himself, breathlessly with relief, over and over, his head against his knees. He tried to rationalise what had just happened. His hair was wet, but it could only be from sweat, not sea water, surely. It was a dream, obviously. A nightmare. He needed to stay awake now until he could get out.

Ricky was so thirsty now that he was too hoarse to shout, so he banged and kicked as hard as he could for as long as he could, hoping that finally he might be heard. He had no idea how much time had passed before he eventually stopped to rest. He was still in a box of silence.

When the whispering started, he was not sure at first whether he was asleep or had imagined it. He clicked on the torch. It flickered, as if the battery or bulb inside was about to stop working. A shadow fluttered on the edge of his vision. He craned his neck towards it but saw nothing beyond the torchlight. A second later, the torch dimmed to a glimmer, then darkness. He clicked the button, shook the torch, banged it against the wall. No change. Either the bulb or battery had died. It didn't matter either way. The darkness was inky black and deep.

'Ricky,' the voice whispered. Ricky's heart jumped. The voice was just at the bottom of his range of hearing, barely present, like a breath of wind.

'What the...' Ricky began.

'Why did you leave me?' said the voice. It was genderless, ageless, hardly audible.

'What?'

'Daddy, why did you leave?' It sounded like two voices in unison, possibly children.

Ricky had left his wife and sons, but that was years ago. They were always arguing; he was better off out of it. He'd moved in with his mother for a bit, and had her house after she died. He saw the kids once a month, when he wasn't busy. He did his bit. It couldn't be them.

'The water is so cold,' it whispered.

'Who is this? Rahim? Nigel? What are you doing?'

'We sank beneath the waves.'

'This isn't funny.'

'Play the game. Play the game. Play the game,' it repeated, like a diminishing echo.

Ricky felt a dull, heavy vibration as gears, cog, pulleys, the nervous system of machinery, began to move. With a lurch, the lift descended. Ricky felt an acceleration and got to his feet. He braced himself, one hand pressed against each facing wall. In gradual, faltering increments, the lift heaved itself to a stop. Ricky tried the door. It swung open heavily, like a coffin lid.

Stepping out onto concrete steps, Ricky felt along the wall for the emergency light switch that he knew would be there. He opened the unlocked panel and pulled the lever. He had worked with similar things on other stations so much that finding it in the darkness was no inconvenience. If it didn't work, however, he knew he would be lost.

The cabling that ran along the walls and ceilings

were fortunately still supplying power. The lights came on and Ricky could see he was on the platform. At least, it was the concrete base of what the platform would have become if it had been completed. The wall curved into the roof above, down to the far side of the track, black with grime but unadorned by any decoration. No theatre posters on this station.

Piles of rubble, discarded bits of wood and tile, unidentifiable detritus wrapped up in blue plastic, were arranged either side of the steps. They had no doubt been there for decades, waiting for a collection that never came.

A sound like metal falling against metal tumbled down the tunnel. Ricky's eyes were drawn to the origin of the sound, which was far into the tunnel, along the rails, where the line of electric lights petered out. Something was moving in the darkness.

'Who's there?' he called.

No answer.

'Rahim? Is that you? For God's sake, mate, it's gone on long enough. I'm sorry if I was... I'm sorry, right?'

No answer.

This time, the wordless whisper in the far darkness almost sounded like a laugh. It wasn't Rahim. Ricky hoisted one tool bag on his shoulder, the other at his feet. More to embolden himself than to show defiance to anyone who might be lurking, he called out into the tunnel.

'Listen, I've come down too far. I'm supposed to check on the telephone line on another level. But while I'm here, I might as well see if I can detect the fault on the wall phone here. Once I've done that, I'll find the stairs and I'll be on my way.' Ricky hoped it gave the right mix of bravado and reasonableness. There was, of course, no response.

Ricky scanned the length of the wall, from one end of the platform to the other, searching for a junction box or telephone. He found what looked like the right cabling that ended in a rectangular metal box at just below head height. It was locked, needing a hexagonal key to open it. Ricky found one in his toolkit and tried it. That unlocked it and, with the stiffness of a box that hadn't been touched in years, it opened.

An old-fashioned wired telephone receiver was inside, sitting in its cradle. Ricky picked it up and put it to his ear. There was a crackle of static.

'Hello?' Ricky said.

The crackle turned into a laugh, faint but distinct.

'Who's there?'

'We are.'

'Who?'

'The abandoned. The forgotten. The dead. The suffocated. The drowned.' The voice trailed off into static.

Ricky was about to answer with some indignant abuse when he noticed that the spiral wire that ran from the receiver terminated nowhere. It was not connected to anything, a loose wire hanging in the dank air.

'I've got to find the stairs,' Ricky decided.

There were two routes to the stairwell. One was blocked by rubble. The other involved walking down the track to the next unfinished piece of platform, from which there was a corridor to the stairwell. It was circuitous, but it was Ricky's only option. Reattaching the receiver would be a relatively easy job, but there was no way he was going to hang around any longer than he needed to. Ricky resolved to get out, even if it cost him his job.

In theory, any moment now a train could come thundering down the line, heading to Golders Green, but it wouldn't be stopping and he wouldn't be noticed, so he had to dismiss that as a hope. He just had to risk being on the tracks for the hundred metres of tunnel between the incomplete slabs of concrete that passed for platforms.

Being one of the few railways electrified on a four-rail system, as Ricky knew, the Underground held hidden dangers for anyone who didn't know where to step. The third rail was electrified. Usually it was outside the two running rails but sometimes between them. Ricky couldn't tell for sure which was which in the poorly illuminated gloom, and he was about to lose all light by stepping into the tunnel. The lights began to dim.

Taking a deep breath, Ricky stepped down onto the track. He kept close to the curving wall, in order to avoid stepping near to any rail at all for as long as he possibly could. His footsteps were uncertain and light, as he tried to make as much progress as quickly as possible.

Something heavier seemed to be making footsteps behind him. He paused, and the steps, like heavy boots, grew louder, as if coming closer. The whispers returned, swirling about his head. Many voices, discordant, but great in number, were whispering over and over, 'Abandoned. Forgotten. Alone.'

As Ricky's eyes adjusted to the darkness in the

tunnel, shapes began to form before his eyes. A crowd of figures, blurred and blended with shadow, stood on the tracks, facing him. Their faces were blank and empty. Flashes of orange showed that some were wearing life jackets. Some were dripping wet. Ricky gasped and turned away.

Before him, between him and the end of the tunnel, were other shapes. His wife and children, carrying battered suitcases, the children tear-stained, his wife angry. 'We couldn't pay the rent,' hissed the whispering voices. 'You left us. Abandoned. Forgotten. Alone.'

In desperation, Ricky made to go back, but behind him, between him and the lift, were shapes that shimmered and glistened in the vague and stifling air. Unspeakably amorphous and distorted, creatures with limbs bending at anarchic angles moved towards him. Drooling, their mouths whispered the words that had followed him. 'Abandoned. Forgotten. Alone.'

It took until the next shift came on for a lineman to be sent down to look for Ricky. Nigel had assumed he had slacked off, and Rahim had been the one to alert the next shift and suggest that they check. No one had noticed that the fault hadn't been reported back until the shift change. When he was found, crouched on the floor of the lift with the door open, he was unconscious.

It had already taken hours for one man to descend the stairwell, so by the time Ricky had been brought to the surface, there was little emergency services could do to bring him round. The report stated that Ricky passed away quietly of an undiagnosed heart condition in the ambulance on the way to hospital.

The medics in the ambulance would only talk in hushed tones afterwards of how Ricky died screaming, eyes wide open, pointing at the corner of the ambulance at unseen monsters.

That August Bank Holiday, whilst Ricky died of shock in an ambulance, an Iraqi man drowned after attempting to reach England by swimming across the English Channel. Other deaths due to people falling from dinghies into the icy waters were reported that month. That week, the number of people attempting to reach the UK in boats in 2019 reached a thousand, nearly three hundred of them in August alone. The Daily Telegraph called it the "summer of chaos".

North End tube station was locked up for another year, and the lift was never used again.

SUMMER'S LEASE

Mike was not sure that going camping at a music festival with a girl he had just met was the wisest decision that he had ever made, but it was certainly the bravest. His friend Kathryn, on the phone from university in Edinburgh, had encouraged him to take that leap. Once upon a different time, Mike and Kathryn might have become an item, but after she lost her Dad at Christmas, it wasn't ever going to be on the cards, especially as she decided to close the house up, put it on the market, and do her postgraduate research in Scotland.

It was a rainy day in Bruges when Mike met Summer. It was a warm August, but the rain brought a welcome break in the heat, and they ended up sharing a shop doorway for shelter from a sudden downpour. They got talking. Both were backpacking across Europe for a few weeks, but heading in different directions. They hung out together for a few days, got as close as Mike would dare, and close enough for Summer to invite him along to the Season's End Music Festival in Bristol.

A few bands that they both knew were playing; some of them were unsigned, so it was a good way to show some support. Finding someone who was into the same sort of left-field music as him was a major part of Mike's attraction to Summer. What she found attractive in him, he had no idea, but he wasn't going to argue with the offer of an end-of-season adventure. Summer picked him up from the train station in Bristol in her second-hand Ford Fiesta, and they camped in a cosy two-man tent in a muddy field next to the festival.

Nobody ever seemed to know what season September belonged to. Mike always associated it with sitting in the hot layers of school uniform at the start of the new term, getting changed into his Arsenal top when he got home, and charging off down the park with his mates and a football until it was time to go home. Autumn wouldn't really start for at least another month. He wouldn't be kicking through piles of fallen leaves in the park until November. Now, he was in his twenties and football was less of an obsession.

When he met Summer, she sparkled with good humour and an openness that made him feel immediately at ease. Her red hair clung to her forehead with the rain, her curls bouncing down to her shoulders in a neat crop top and shorts. Now, in the evening of a muggy September, she clung to her chunky cardigan, ripped jeans and Wolf Alice t-shirt.

The last band of the night was finishing the encore as Mike and Summer headed back to their tent. Arm in arm, she made him hold her as she swung herself over every puddle she could find. The challenge was to avoid splashing mud, but of course she failed and they were both plastered by the time they reached the encampment. Other people were either diving into their tents together or congregating in groups to share cans and bottles. The air was already filling with sweet-smelling smoke. Mike was a little nervous: he wasn't much of a smoker, and he'd already had his fill of expensive fizzy lager in plastic cups for one day. It was fortunate, then, that Summer had other plans.

'Come over the hill with me,' she said. 'There's a campfire with a storyteller over there, apparently. We can snuggle up, toast some marshmallows…' She looked up at him with big, hopeful eyes and a smile that made it seem like the most exciting offer in history. She could have offered him anything in that moment, and he would have said yes.

'Yeah, sure,' he said.

Summer grabbed his hand and led the way past the camping area, over the brow of a hill towards a copse that seemed to stand alone in the next open field. Smoke was wisping up through the trees.

'That's the campfire,' Summer said, pointing. 'Come on.'

When they reached the campfire, half a dozen other people, all about the same age and in various states of home-knitted clothing and hats, were sitting in a rough circle on the grass. Cross-legged at the focal point of the curve was the storyteller. She was an older woman, possibly in her sixties or even older, but fit and wiry, with long grey hair in plaits. She was dressed in an approximation of traditional Native American clothing, with a patterned blanket across her lap and a beaded necklace that looked as if it could be genuine. Mike took it in but didn't really care. This was either going to be cringeworthy or a bit of fun. Either way, he was experiencing it with a girl unlike any, in spirit and demeanour, that he had ever met before.

The older lady beckoned for them to sit across from her, on the other side of the crackling fire. 'Welcome,' she said. 'You're just in time. Please sit. I'll collect your money during the interval. Now, my name is Ms Rainbird. But you can call me Gladys.'

Some of the audience tittered. 'Yes, I know,' she sighed. 'My grandmother is Native American. She fell in love with an English sailor, left the reservation and settled here in Bristol. But she brought with her an ancient heritage, and a great many stories from a great many tribes across North America that she passed down to my mother and me. Granny Rainbird and Mum are long gone, but I sit here now with you around the fire to share those stories.

The audience was quiet now, listening. Summer sat with Mike, holding his head, enraptured by the old lady. The light from the flames danced across Summer's cheeks and her eyes glistened in the firelight. A handful of teenagers, who had probably arrived together, made their non-apologies and left, in search of something 'a bit less boring'. The older woman ignored them, and settled herself on a cushion, ready to begin.

'In the ancient legends of the Seneca tribe in the northeast woodlands of North America, there is a story about the change in seasons. Here we are, in September, warmer than expected, on the cusp between summer and autumn, but this is a story about Spring and Winter. In many traditions, the seasons take on human form,' she said.

Mike nudged Summer, as if she needed reminding that she was named after a season. She winked back at him. He felt as if his heart jumped out of his body in that split second. There really was something special about this girl. Her eyes danced with a mischievous warmth that made her so different to anyone he had met before.

Ms Rainbird continued, 'Far back in the past, not long after the world was first created, there was an old man. He had a long, white beard and carried his age with him wherever he went. His steps made the ground hard and dry. His breath stopped the rivers flowing. Plants shrivelled away. Animals ran away from him. The old man lived in a house of ice and snow. His only visitor was the North Wind, who would sit with him and boast about his plans to make the world even colder.'

'I think I know a few politicians like that,' joked someone else in the audience. Summer shushed him.

Ms Rainbird raised a single finger. 'One morning, the old man saw that his land of ice and snow was starting to thaw. The North Wind shrugged and told the old man that he was off. He flew off further north until he found deeper snow and thicker ice. The old man was alone, but he was defiant. He was sure his house of ice and snow would stay forever.'

Gladys Rainbird paused to pass a little felt hat to the person on her right. This was for them to put in their payment. It was just five pounds, but another small group baulked at this and took it as an opportunity to leave, probably attracted by the deep bass sounds coming from a bluetooth speaker back over the hill. The hat came around to Mike and Summer. Mike dropped in a ten-pound note and passed it on. By the time the hat came back to the storyteller, there were just half a dozen people left around the campfire. She put the hat to one side without looking at the contents. Mike guessed that she was used to ending up with a more selective audience.

'What happened to the old man?' asked one of the others, a man in shorts and a neatly sculpted beard. His wife was dozing off beside him, leaning against his shoulder.

'I was about to get to that,' the storyteller replied. 'After some time, there was a knock on the old man's door. He ignored it. The knocking turned into heavy, splintering blows, as if someone was hacking at the door with an axe. Pieces of ice started falling from the door, the walls and the ceiling. He shouted for his attacker to go away, but it was too late. The door of ice shattered. Standing in the doorway was a young man.'

'Was he an axe murderer?' asked the man in shorts, laughing at his own failed attempt at a joke. Everyone, including his wife, ignored him.

'Without waiting to be invited in,' the storyteller continued, 'the young man came in and sat down opposite the old man. Now, the old man had a fire much like ours here, but his flames were as cold as frost. When the young man, dressed in green, poked at the fire with his stick of green wood, it became hot. The flames turned from white to yellow and heat filled the house. The walls began to melt and the old man began to sweat. In a panic, the old man interrogated the young man and threatened him with his icy breath.'

The man in shorts laughed, but there was an unkind

edge to it. The storyteller shot him a glance. The man's wife whispered something harsh in his ear and got up to leave. She apologised to the old woman and left, dragging her husband behind her. Mike could just about pick out the word 'embarrassment' as she scolded her husband.

Undeterred, Gladys Rainbird stood up, holding herself in a stance like the old man, arms spread wide in simulated anger. 'I make the animals and birds fly from me in fear! I make the land hard and cold! I am the freezing force that rules this world!'

She then mimed the younger man, hands on hips, confident and mocking, saying, 'I'm not scared of you. Haven't you worked out who I am yet? I bring warmth. I make the plants grow and the snow melt! The birds and animals flock around me. My friend is the South Wind, and she comes to blow you away!' And she acted great gusts of wind, blowing air from her puffed-out cheeks.

'Phew,' she said. 'That took it out of me. I'll sit down to finish.' She sat, then continued, 'The old man with the white beard shrank away and melted to nothing like a candle. His house collapsed and a beautiful meadow full of wild flowers bloomed in its place.'

The audience applauded. 'That was an old Native American legend about how Spring defeated Winter. If you think about it, they go through the same cycle every year. We'll take a little break now, then I'll tell you the Pawnee story of Coyote and the Rock.'

Drawn by the sounds of merriment over the hill, the remainder of the audience took this cue to go, thanking the old lady but being 'really tired' but actually wanting to dance the rest of the night away. Soon, only Mike and

Summer were left.

Ms Rainbird was sipping tea from a flask when Summer approached her. The old lady nodded. 'It's a pleasure to meet you,' said Summer.

'You too. You're… different this year.'

'So are you.'

Mike stood frozen for a moment. The hairs on the back of his neck prickled. Something wasn't right. What did they mean?

'Do you two know each other?' Mike asked warily.

The old lady sipped her tea. Summer turned to him and smiled the same disarming smile that had attracted him to her in the first place. He immediately felt reassured, even before she spoke. 'Sort of,' she said. Then she turned back to the old lady and asked, 'Can I tell him?'

'I don't see why not. There aren't any rules. He might not like it though.'

'What? What's the big secret?' Mike was worried now.

Summer took his hands in hers and looked him straight in the eyes. They were close enough to kiss. Her breath was light, like flowers. 'Mike, it's been a very long time since I last fell in love with a man,' she began.

'You love me? We hadn't actually said it, but I…'

She shushed him gently, then continued. 'That legend about Spring and Summer has some truth in it. Had you wondered where Summer and Autumn were in the story?'

'Oh, very funny. You had me going for a minute then. Yeah, I get it. You're Summer. Does that make Gladys…'

'Yes, indeed. I'm Autumn. Pleased to meet you,' said the old lady, turning to face Mike.

'So, you're what, ghosts?' he laughed.

'Yes'.

There was a slight chill in the air. From far off, the breeze brought the faint smell of a bonfire. Leaves rustled in the trees. Mike had to admit, it suddenly felt very autumnal.

Summer squeezed his hands tightly. 'I can see you're sceptical. It doesn't really matter whether you think it's true, but I want you to understand what happens next. Every year, as the seasons turn, our paths cross. Winter gives way bitterly to Spring. Spring is always joyous when I take his place because he knows he'll be back next year. There's me and Autumn, and later on, Autumn gets frozen out by Winter. She hates him.'

'Well, I'm always really ready for a long sleep by then, but he's a curmudgeonly old bastard. I'm always suspicious of people who prefer the winter months. Christmas is no excuse,' said the old lady that Mike now knew to be Autumn.

Mike saw the flaw in the little role-play going on in front of him. 'If that's true,' he said, 'then Autumn here has to kill you, Summer. Is that right?'

Autumn and Summer exchanged glances nervously.

Summer said, 'Well, this is the thing. You see, I've fallen in love. With you, just to clarify again. I'm not ready to go yet. You know how sometimes summer doesn't seem to end in September and it stays warm for quite a while?'

'Uh, yeah...'

'Well, that's me hanging on a bit longer. But now,

I feel the leaves are ready to fall and become brown. Bare feet on lush green grass will give way to boots crunching on those brown leaves. I'm sad because, well, like Shakespeare said, "Summer's lease hath all too short a date". He was clever, that one.' Summer placed her hand on the back of Mike's neck and pulled him in for a kiss. Her lips were sweet and soft.

Summer stepped back and took Autumn's hand. They stood side by side, facing Mike. 'No, don't...' he began, still unsure what to believe.

Autumn's voice was soothing. 'We aren't like Spring and Winter. For us, it's not combative.'

There were tears in Summer's eyes. 'I really did love you,' she said.

The light from the campfire flicked shadows over them as the two women seemed suddenly indistinct. Mike rubbed his eyes. He could no longer tell where one woman ended and the other began. He closed his eyes, rubbed them again. When he opened them and refocused, there was one woman standing in front of him.

She looked like Summer in many ways. She had the same smile; her eyes glistened in the same way; but her hair hung in plaits and she wore the clothes that Autumn wore.

'Summer?' he said.

'Autumn,' she replied. 'Come on, let's go and get a drink.'

HARVEST

O ctober began wet and continued that way, with the jet stream dragging with it bands of rain. By the middle of the month, harvest really should have been over. The farm's wheat crop had been harvested, leaving stubble already seeded with next year's crop. The adjacent field was full with maize that towered like scarecrows and should really have been cut down by now, but since it was a variety that was being sold this year for silage, it was being left to the last minute. There was plenty to do with apples, carrots, beetroot and, of course, pumpkins in the coming weeks.

The maize harvest had never been quite this late before. It was now 13th October, thirteen days after the deadline that his father used to set for himself. When his father ran the farm, before it was sold off, he had rigid timelines for everything. Even Keith had to run to a timetable. Since his father died, he'd tried to follow his example, but sometimes he failed, like this year.

Keith's father used to be the owner of the farm. Now, Keith was more like an employee; the farm itself had been in his family for a long time, but was now owned by Pasturage Estates. His job these days was to stay in the old farmhouse and run the day-to-day operations. With staff shortages, this meant that driving the combine harvester had fallen to him. The farmhouse was only really a place for him to stay: it was a tumbledown cottage kept only for sentimental reasons. The business side of the farm itself was run from an office building near the main road. He tried not to think about the future of his work: for now, all he had to concentrate on tomorrow was the maize, and the harvester, and getting back on track with what his father would have expected of him.

But first, it was late, and he had to sleep.

When Keith woke, he glanced at his phone to see the time. It was thirteen minutes past one. Still the middle of the night, not even approaching morning. Keith quickly realised that it was a noise that had disturbed his sleep. At first, it sounded like static from an untuned radio. But he hadn't had a radio like that since he was a child. He wasn't sure they even made them anymore - everything was digital now.

Looking out the window, in the moonlight, he could see the field of maize. In the far distance, a combine harvester was rolling through the crop. Was someone stealing farm machinery in the middle of the night? By the time he had rung the police or anyone else, it would be too late. There was a security guard on site, but his job was to patrol the buildings and entrance from the road. There wouldn't be any point in pulling him away, especially as he was a bit overweight. Keith made this calculation as he leapt down the stairs three at a time.

Still in his pyjamas, Keith pulled on his Wellington boots at the back door, grabbed a torch and ran towards the field. With the beam bouncing in front of him, leading the way, he thought that he should really have taken the shotgun down from its place on the wall. Too late now.

The maize - tall, majestic ears of corn reaching higher than his five-feet-nine-inches frame - seemed to close in on him as he plunged into the field. There was a reason that many farms turned the crop into a maze. The maize maze offered no straight way through. Keith tried to head towards the sound.

The churning, softly roaring sound of the combine harvesting the stalks, leaves and all into the thresher was closer now. Keith pushed on in a straight line, hacking the plants to either side of him as he neared the machine.

Keith swung the torch towards what he expected to be the green John Deere machine that he used every week on the farm. Instead, the light passed through an older harvester. Ethereal, as if it were an image superimposed on the scene, the yellow machine was flaked with rust, but he knew it. It had belonged to his father. But surely it was now rotting in a barn, ready for scrap?

The reel of the machine was turning, driving the crop through to the cutter bar, the metal arms of the reel bats rotating to lift the maize. The knife sections mounted on the cutter bar were merciless, throwing the crop through to the threshing drum. Inside, the rasp bars separated the grain from the straw and the chaff just as easily as a modern machine. This machine was there but not there, unloading harvested grain into the trailer attached behind, despite being intangible. It was nearly transparent in the moonlit darkness, Keith's torch beam passing through into nothingness.

Keith watched helplessly as the machine passed him. Already half way through, it kept going back and forth until it had passed back and forth along the field thirteen times, leaving rows as neat and straight as the John Deere would have done.

Before his astonished gaze, the combine harvester stopped. Keith's eyes were finally drawn upwards to the cab. A man was sitting at the wheel, grey at the temples, balding, slightly overweight from the excess of beer and food that eventually overwhelmed his heart. The man, as gossamer in substance as the machine, smiled down at Keith and waved genially.

The man, wispy and impalpable, was Keith's father.

As Keith waved back, tears in his eyes, the ghosts of man and machine faded into the moonlight.

All that was left behind was a very solid trailer containing a heap of harvested maize, ready for silage.

Later that morning, once the sun was in the sky, Keith resumed work. At the end of the day, he left thirteen rows unharvested, then he went early to bed and waited for thirteen minutes past one to arrive.

KENILWORTH DARK

Kathryn Dark sat opposite her PhD supervisor whilst he browsed through a sheaf of papers. His office was crammed with similar papers secured with elastic bands. Others were boxed and labelled by hand. One box was marked out as containing 'floppy discs'. Kathryn was willing to bet Tim hadn't even glanced at that box in twenty years. The shelves were distressingly disorganised, chaotically crammed, but Tim's desk was almost clear: just a laptop, wireless mouse and the bundle that he was currently leafing through. He was someone who was efficient in the moment, but beneath the iceberg was a different story.

Kathryn knew better than to interrupt him whilst he was reading, so she relaxed, looking out of the window at the Edinburgh vista, a panorama of buildings ancient and contemporary. The city was a beautiful place, even when viewed through the November drizzle. It felt like home now. After doing her degree here, then her MA, and now her PhD, it felt like somewhere she might stay. She was equally glad that she had gone home to Dad at Christmas, although it ended with such sadness. Throwing herself back into her research, getting some bar work, and making new friends in the city, had all helped in the grieving process.

Tim's Inverness accent rolled softly as he muttered to himself, seemingly giving a running commentary on Kathryn's notes. He was an established academic, fit and trim for a man in his early forties. He had penned a few books on psychology, including a reappraisal of Carl Jung that was required reading on Kathryn's undergraduate degree. She had sought him out as her supervisor once she was sure what she wanted her PhD to be, convinced he would be supportive of her ideas.

'This is a bit of a mess, really, isn't it?' Tim said, finally.

'Thanks, Tim. I tried really hard to cultivate that impression,' Kathryn replied, masking her sudden embarrassment.

'Yes, I can see. Okay, let's recap where we are, shall we?'

'Okay, well...'

'How are you doing?'

The question was unexpected. Kathryn expected to talk about the work only. 'What do you mean?' she asked, wary.

'Well, I know you lost your Dad last Christmas...'

'You were very kind about that.'

'I know. I'm a sweetheart. What I mean is, how are you personally doing at the moment? Some might think it's an unprofessional question, but I have to know what my students' wellbeing is like so that we can have productive conversations about timescales for the thesis, that sort of thing. It's important, I think.' He wasn't smiling, but there was genuine kindness in his green-blue eyes.

Kathryn adjusted her position in the chair. She was suddenly uncomfortable. 'Thank you, Tim. Um… well, I sold Dad's house. That went through a few weeks ago. It sold quite quickly, I suppose. No chain. I'd already come back up to Edinburgh, got a nice flat.'

'I gather you've picked up some bar work?'

'Yep. I do some shifts at The Jazz Basement, and one of the coffee shops in the old town. It covers the rent, but like I say, the house is sold so…'

'That's good. Because if you let the research just consume you and you don't have a life outside of it, that's not helpful.'

'I've made some new friends too. Miles is nice, and there's…'

With a slight handwave, Tim cut her off. He knew enough now. 'Okay, that's good. So, on to the topic of your thesis…' He started flicking through the papers again and went quiet for a slightly longer moment than Kathryn was comfortable with. Finally, he said, 'Pitch it to me again. It's about the psychology of believing in ghosts, right?'

'Sort of. It's more like the psychology of experiencing them. I'm not saying ghosts are real in the traditional sense, but there are some commonalities in the experiences that people report, and a crossover with some incidents of psychosis.' She was aware that she was starting to ramble and straightened her back in the chair, forcing herself to get to the point. 'So, according to Jung, as we know, the collective unconscious is made up of archetypes. Myths and symbols, including things like ghosts, are incredibly similar in cultures around the world, both historically and in contemporary reports.'

'So, your idea is that the collective unconscious is made up of archetypes. That's not new, but you're saying that somehow this explains what people report as ghost sightings?'

'Not just sightings. Deeper experiences. I've talked to a few people this year about things they've experienced, and possibly I experienced something myself. I'm not saying these are ghosts per se, but maybe there's something in the collective unconscious worth exploring. What's going on when we think we're encountering ghosts? Is it a waking dream state? What's happening in the brain? I think this could help in developing new approaches for psychotherapy.'

'Hmm. Maybe. Jung is all well and good. But is there anything new to say?' Tim sat back in his chair. Behind him, on the shelf, a few copies of his own book on Jung were haphazardly stacked. Kathryn couldn't help but glance at them.

'Well, it's not just Jung. So, I've been reading Melanie Klein. You know, her thoughts on how the struggle between the life and death instincts carry on throughout life struck a chord with me. The life instinct drives us towards creation; the death instinct sends us the other way towards destruction. Life itself is striving against death. I think maybe that psychic tension that we all have could explain at least some of the experiences that people report as supernatural. If we understand that better...'

'You could make links with cognitive psychology too, I suppose.'

'Yes!'

Tim handed Kathryn's pile of papers back to her, now all much messier than when she gave them to him. 'Okay,' he said. 'What's next then?'

'I'll be heading back down to England for a week, I think.'

'What for?'

She hesitated, and blushed, involuntarily revealing her embarrassment. She told herself that she shouldn't give in to that feeling, as this was at the core of what she wanted to do with this PhD. This would be the real test of it. If Tim didn't like it, then it would never be viable anyway. She said, 'I'm going to a town in Warwickshire called Kenilworth. There's someone there I've been talking to online. I want to look into the phenomenon of doppelgangers. There are lots of documented cases of people thinking they've seen their doubles. Folklore has it that they could be some sort of ghost. I want to look into what might be going on psychologically in such cases.'

'Okay, let me know how it goes.' Tim was impossible to read now. He seemed to be okay with it. Maybe the only person that Kathryn was really doubting was herself.

What Kathryn had neglected to tell Tim was the unsettling feeling that had been following her around for weeks. Three weeks earlier, she had woken in the middle of the night and gone to the bathroom. As she turned to leave after washing her hands, she saw herself out of the corner of her eye. She was still standing in the mirror, face front where her reflection should have been in profile. Kathryn was able to dismiss this as her imagination, half awake, until what happened two nights later.

It was a cold night, with rain pattering against the window, but Kathryn slept soundly until she was suddenly fully awake. She had a sensation of having been asleep, but no sense of how much time had passed, so she checked the time. Thirteen minutes past one in the morning. Assuming that it must be her bladder sending her a message again, she swung her legs on to the floor, ready to stand. Something in her peripheral vision made her stop mid-movement.

At the foot of the bed, wearing the same old t-shirt that she was wearing, Kathryn saw herself. The other Kathryn was sitting on the edge of the bed, facing away towards the en suite bathroom. The apparition was absolutely still, like a still photograph in three dimensions.

Meekly, Kathryn said, 'Hello?' and reached tentatively towards the shape that was unmistakably her. As if the darkness wielded a brush, the other Kathryn was swept away in that moment. Kathryn was alone again.

In the morning, Kathryn once again dismissed the experience as a dream. Being knee-deep in reading about ghosts, hearing Miles's story, and having had a strange experience herself at Christmas, it was hardly surprising. However, she reported for her shift at the coffee shop to be met by an array of surprised faces.

Heading towards the back room to hang up her coat and put on her apron, Kathryn said 'Good morning' to the manager, a middle-aged woman named Esther, and the other barista George, a laid-back fellow student with the most hipsterish beard she had seen in some time. Esther and George exchanged puzzled glances, and Esther gently halted Kathryn, her hand on Kathryn's forearm.

'Where did you go?' Esther asked, her brow furrowed.

Kathryn was more confused. 'What do you mean?' she replied.

'You already arrived about ten minutes ago. Did you go out for something? I didn't see you leave. I thought you were still out back?'

'Er... no.'

'Then, that's weird.'

George joined the conversation. 'I thought it was odd that you didn't say anything. You just breezed past us and went through. I just thought you needed the loo,' he said.

The colour drained from Kathryn's face. Together, they all went into the back room. For anyone to exit, Esther would have been able to see them from her vantage point in the cafe, so whoever it was had to still be there. The room was empty apart from supplies, a cold kettle. The door to the toilet was open, itself empty.

That evening, Kathryn found an online paranormal discussion group and joined a thread about doppelgangers. The consensus seemed to be that they were ghostly doubles. After all, the word translated from German meant "double walker". She dug into examples from folklore, which showed the doppelganger to be an evil omen, a harbinger of doom. They were all either malevolent twins or a ghostly entity. More scientifically, seeing one's own double in the distance could be a sign of schizophrenia or epilepsy. On the face of it, Kathryn was interested in psychopathy rather than the urban legend. However, she found herself drawn to other explanations.

Now, she was nearing the end of her long journey from Scotland. The taxi driver kept carefully to the twenty miles per hour speed limit on the main street of the affluent Warwickshire town of Kenilworth. He pulled into the layby outside the Holiday Inn at the top of the street, Kathryn paid him, and she stepped into Reception with her battered overnight bag hanging off her shoulder.

'Kathryn Dark. I've got a room booked,' she said to the woman at the Reception desk. Whilst she was confirming the booking and issuing the key card, Kathryn asked, 'I've got an appointment to meet someone at... I think he said The - ahem - Virgins and Castle pub? Any idea where it is?'

The woman smiled indulgently. 'It's lovely, actually. A bit of a bloke's pub, but it's lovely. The oldest pub in Kenilworth. It's on High Street, which is in the old part of town. You can walk from here, and in fact you could walk through Abbey Fields - that's the park - as long as it's not too dark by then.' She pointed in the right direction and gave more detailed instructions.

Kathryn thanked her and went up to her room to settle in. She made a cup of tea and sat on the bed to consider what the hell she was doing. Meeting a

161

complete stranger in a pub after meeting him online was everything her parents warned her against. Agreeing to go for a drink with a man she had never met before was everything her friends would think was completely insane. Who the hell did she think she was? This pathetic attempt at a PhD was going to get her laughed out of every academic institution on earth. She thought about cancelling. Her fingers poised over her phone to message the man she was meeting.

'No, don't be an idiot,' she said to herself. 'Buy your own drink. Only talk in the bar. Keep it public. Get a taxi afterwards, on your own. You'll be fine.' She let herself be angry for a moment that this was what every woman had to consider every bloody day.

The pub was cosy and welcoming. Kathryn arrived a few minutes early, ordered herself a Diet Coke and sat at a table near the bar. With her notebook and pen and her phone with the voice recording app open on the table, she felt ready and, possibly, almost professional. She felt sure that "Jimmy Hopkins" was a social media nom de plume, nevertheless this was who she was about to meet.

Presently, a middle-aged man entered. He was unremarkable: grey-haired with a stubbly beard; spectacles that were probably varifocals; a coat zipped up to his chin. Kathryn quickly noticed, to her relief, that he had a woman with him. Her coat was embroidered, much smarter and more expensive. Her straggly grey hair was tied back in a ponytail, her cheeks red from coming in from the cold. It was she who noticed Kathryn first and pointed her out to the man. They came over together and the man extended his hand.

'Kathryn, I assume? I'm Jimmy. This is my wife, Jenny.'

Jimmy and Jenny. Really? Well, it didn't matter. 'Pleased to meet you. Can I get you a drink?' Kathryn replied, starting to get up.

'No, we'll get our own, thanks.' Jenny was already at the bar as he sat down across from Kathryn. 'Hope you don't mind my wife coming. She wanted to make sure I wasn't being scammed. Not that you - I mean, you can never be sure.'

Kathryn laughed with relief. 'No, that's just fine by me. No offence, but making a date to meet a man I've never met in a pub I've never been to is probably not the wisest decision I've ever made. Not that you - you know what I mean?'

Joining them with a pint of Guinness and a glass of red wine, Jenny shook Kathryn's hand warmly. 'You're nervous,' she said.

'Just a bit.'

'Well, we'll try not to drag it out. Jimmy's been desperate to tell anyone who will listen about what happened. He's just glad someone is taking him seriously.'

'Is it alright if I record this?' Kathryn asked.

Jimmy shifted uncomfortably. 'I'd... I don't know. I mean...'

'That's fine,' she replied, putting her phone in her pocket. 'I'll just make notes.'

Jimmy and Jenny nodded their assent. There was an awkward pause. Jenny broke the ice first. 'Kenilworth is quite a haunted town, of course. There's the castle, most famously. But most of those are just stories. What we experienced is quite different and, strangely, not unique, it seems.'

'Yes, I heard. I understand in nineteen-ninety-seven there was a couple who claimed that they were followed by their doppelgangers in Abbey Fields? That's, well, just around the corner, isn't it?'

Jenny nodded. 'Yes. If you turn left out of here, the road becomes Bridge Street and then you can turn into a little walk past St Nicholas' church and it's there in the graveyard that supposedly happened. That area is also haunted by the ghost of a faceless monk. We've never seen him, though.'

'So, what happened to you? If you take it slowly so I can make notes...'

Jenny sat back and sipped her wine. She gestured for her husband to take over. Jimmy took a gulp of his stout, then he began. 'I never used to believe in this stuff, but I've come to realise that ghosts are real. They just aren't what we think they are. In my case, I'm being haunted by myself.'

Kathryn suddenly felt cold. 'What do you mean?' she asked.

'For years now, usually at night-time, I'll get a feeling that someone is behind me. It's like that feeling of someone watching you over your shoulder. But, in my case, whenever I catch a glimpse, it's me. My double. Watching me. Following me. Always a few steps behind, but never quite catching up. By the time I notice it - him - it's already disappearing. It tends to happen when I'm half asleep at home, or when I'm walking. The closest I've come to him actually catching up with me was in the St Nicholas church graveyard. I was on my way back from a mate's house. We'd been out for a curry and went back to his house for a nightcap. A bit of a tradition. Lads' night out. That time, I decided I'd had enough. I waited around the corner, against one of the gravestones, so I could face him. I waited, but he never came. He'd gone. That was a few weeks ago, at thirteen minutes past one in the morning. I don't know why I took note of the time, but I did.'

Jimmy seemed relieved to get his story out. Kathryn set her notebook to one side, and replied, 'I… don't know. It's probably a coincidence, but…' and she explained what had happened to her; her own doppelganger waking her at thirteen minutes past one in the morning. When she got to the end of her story, Jimmy looked at her with tears in his eyes. Kathryn couldn't tell whether it was from relief that someone finally believed him or out of empathy for what she felt. Jenny just nodded sagely, as if she already knew.

'There's more,' Jenny said, gently squeezing her husband's hand. 'He's been waking up at one-thirteen on the dot every single morning since then, every time seeing himself sitting at the end of the bed.'

'He just looks at me so coldly, as if… as if I'm some sort of specimen. Then he's gone, and I'm…' Jimmy began, then stopped as he choked down a sob.

Jenny said, 'He won't go to the doctor, but I know one theory is that these could be hallucinations. I mean, Jimmy's had some mental health issues.' She squeezed his hand again.

'Just anxiety and depression, the usual stuff,' he shrugged.

Kathryn drained her Diet Coke. 'Can I get you another drink?' she asked.

'No,' said Jenny. 'But I have an idea. If you're around for a couple of days, it's the fireworks display at Kenilworth Castle tomorrow. I work part-time there, so I'll be helping out with a bit of stewarding, doing the car park, that sort of thing. Why don't you come along? There's always a huge crowd and a good display, provided it doesn't rain too much. We can talk again then, maybe have some dinner when the display's finished. I'd like to see if you can help us get to the bottom of what's happening to Jimmy, and we can give you some more information for your thesis.'

'If that's alright?'

Jimmy nodded, finishing his pint. 'Yes, of course. I think I just need to go and get my head down now for the night.'

They shook hands, and the couple left. Kathryn stayed for another drink on her own, this time ordering a large glass of wine. With her head buried in her notes and phone, nobody bothered her, which was what she needed. She texted Miles, just to let him know where she was and what she was doing. He had a concert, so probably wouldn't see the text until later. She also texted her friend Mike. They had made tentative plans to meet up again over Christmas, as it would be a year since her father died, but he was difficult to get hold of. The last she knew, he'd met a girl when he was backpacking in Europe.

She was eager for gossip, but he was being cagey. Typical.

The last orders bell rang before Kathryn realised. She had completely lost track of time. As she packed up her belongings into her handbag, the barman came over to wipe the table. Kathryn asked, 'Sorry to bother you. Where can I find the St Nicholas Church - the walk through the graveyard?'

He looked at her with some concern. 'It's just up the hill a bit. You'll see a little sign. It's well illuminated. But I wouldn't then walk across Abbey Fields on your own in the dark, if I were you. Once you've gone through the church, you can cut through the car park and then walk along the main road back to your hotel, if that's what you need to do.'

Kathryn took his advice, and quickly found the pathway through the graveyard. Built from red sandstone, the Gothic church towered over the ruins of St Mary's Abbey, the remains of a Norman and Gothic structure supposedly haunted by the faceless monk. Graves were haphazardly laid out in the churchyard either side of the path, some undisturbed for centuries. Others had long ago been unattended and all that remained were lumps of stone weathered to uneven molars, the names long disappeared. Kathryn was tempted to look more closely, curious about some of the names and dates, but decided to leave that until daylight.

Further away from the path, shadows hugged the gravestones, the branches of a tree the only movement in the wind. Spots of rain pecked at the ground. As Kathryn turned from the sleeping places of the dead towards the car park that stood parallel to the murky pitch-blackness of Abbey Fields, she saw a fox dart across the path. It was quickly swallowed by shadow, seeking its prey in the hedgerows and bushes.

The only sounds Kathryn could hear, aside from the distant traffic, were the pitter-patter of raindrops and her own footsteps. But wait. A sound like footsteps was behind her, between her steps. Each time she took a step, it echoed behind her, the sound of a woman's shoe touching the tarmac.

Kathryn felt a presence. It was like the feeling of being watched, but colder and more unfeeling, as if she were being judged. She turned, fists clenched, ready to face whatever she had to face.

In her peripheral vision, a figure dashed between the stones and a tree towards the ruins of the abbey. The figure was in the shape of a woman, something like a handbag flapping from its shoulder. Kathryn gasped. This was too coincidental to be true. Had she really seen it?

Running, she followed the phantom. The shade was just ahead of her, half hidden by the low branches of a tree. It was her silhouette; it had the same curve of her body, the same flow of her hair. It was now still. She stepped closer. Features were becoming more distinct: her lips, curved in a sneer; her eyes, staring blankly; her hands, fingers spread in supplication.

Unbidden, a scream broiled from deep within Kathryn. Recovering her breath, she wiped the spittle from her mouth with the back of her hand. Teeth gritted, biting down on her fear, she said, 'What do you want?'

Her doppelganger put its hands together as if in

prayer, its face growing grey and less distinct, like smoke. 'What do you want?' Kathryn repeated. A gust of wind through the trees and a spray of the thickening rain swept the apparition away, dissipating into the darkness.

Back in her hotel room, Kathryn took a tiny bottle of vodka from the mini-bar and downed it in one go. She sat on the closed seat of the toilet for what felt like several minutes, head in her hands, whilst she tried to control her breathing. She mustn't let herself panic. Needing noise to distract and drown out her thoughts, she turned on the room's television, selected a news channel and increased the volume as much as she dared. With the voices blaring in the background, she took a shower. She stayed under the water long after she was clean, washing away the night.

Kathryn awoke abruptly. The television images still glared, but the room was otherwise in darkness and silent. She remembered she had muted it before she laid down in her dressing gown. She had fallen asleep there and then, but now she was awake. She sat up, adrenalin surging, and looked around the room.

The clock showed that the time was thirteen minutes after one o'clock. Kathryn waited, but she was alone. She waited, alone, until sleep finally claimed her.

The following day was punctuated by rain. Kathryn spent some time wandering around the town's charity shops. She found two excellent bookshops, one of which was stacked high with second hand books and she spent most of the afternoon browsing, and chatting with the owner. She avoided being too specific about why she was in Kenilworth, but it kept her mind away from the previous night. She took a recommendation for a place to have a coffee, and sat there until it was time to go to the castle. The scone that she ordered went untouched, and the coffee grew cold, as she stared through the window into the rain and jumble of people going about their business.

At the appointed time, Kathryn walked across the road, past the library, and followed a leafy road down and up a hill until she reached Kenilworth Castle. Crowds were already assembling within its walls, ready for the firework display that took place in its grounds every year. She scoured the car park for Jenny, looking for anyone wearing the hi-vis security jacket that marked out the volunteers.

Eventually, she saw Jenny, in her embroidered coat, under an umbrella, talking to a woman wearing the yellow hi-vis. As Kathryn approached, Jenny hugged her friend, who then departed towards the entrance. As she passed Kathryn, she said, 'Be gentle with her.'

Confused, Kathryn put out her hand in greeting. Jenny took it under hers and held on. Her face was clear, even a little defiant. She was wearing no make-up and the redness under her eyes betrayed the fact that she had been crying. 'I could have just messaged you,' she said, 'but I needed to get out of the house. Besides, I have friends here.'

'What happened?' Kathryn asked, only just now noticing that Jimmy was not with her.

'Last night, Jimmy woke up in the middle of the

night. He was staring at something in the far corner of the room. He was reaching out to whatever it was, and then he collapsed. Heart attack.'

'I'm sorry. Is he…'

Jenny nodded. 'He's dead.'

'Oh, I'm so sorry.' Kathryn embraced the woman whom she hardly knew. Jenny hugged back. Kathryn hesitated before asking, but she knew she had to. 'What time did it happen?'

'Thirteen minutes past one in the morning.'

The firework displays dazzled and sparkled overhead, booming their spectacle through the rain and into the shadows.

EPILOGUE

Mike returned to the table with two coffees and two pieces of cake. Kathryn greedily took hers and stabbed it with a fork. Munching on the first bite of lemon drizzle cake, she blew him a kiss. The crumbs narrowly missed his plate. She laughed so much she nearly choked. Swallowing hard, she took a sip of her coffee. Too hot. She winced and put it back down.

'That's karma, that is.'

'Yeah, sorry. I'm just so hungry.'

They both tucked into their slices of cake more carefully now, pausing to sip coffee and chat. Mike looked around the cafe. They had both grown up in this town, but never bothered much with this cafe when they were younger. He felt old, although they were both still in their twenties.

'Anyway, here's to your Dad,' he said, raising his cup in a toast. They clinked coffee cups and drank.

'Can't believe it's already been nearly a year. Where did 2019 go?' Kathryn replied.

'Just the ghost of it left, eh?'

Kathryn's face fell, her eyes straight and serious. 'Don't joke about that.'

'Sorry. But it has been a weird year, hasn't it?'

'If only you knew. Anyway, tell me about this

girlfriend of yours.'

'It was... a seasonal thing. Great while it lasted. Maybe... maybe I'll see her again next year, who knows,' he shrugged.

Those serious eyes narrowed now. 'You and your secrets,' she said. 'What are you doing for Christmas Day, then? At home with Mum?'

'Yeah. Might as well. You're welcome to join us, you know. She would love to have you over.' It was an enthusiastic offer, and Kathryn did like Mike's mother. She used to make the whole gang of kids milkshakes whenever they bundled into Mike's house.

'No thanks,' she said. 'I'll go back up to Scotland.'

'On your own, though?'

'Somehow, I don't think I will be.'

'Well then, let's have one more toast before you go,' Mike said, raising his cup again. 'To 2020. Let's hope it'll be a great year.'

'Well, it couldn't be any worse.'

ABOUT THE AUTHOR

Jason Cobley was born in 1968. He lives in Warwickshire with his wife and daughter, and works as a teacher.

He is not a ghost yet.

ACKNOWLEDGEMENTS

Thank you to Izzy, who helped come up with many
of the ideas that became parts of this book.

Thank you to everyone who has supported my writing
over the years, especially when you didn't have to.

Thank you to the members of the Breakthrough
Book Collective, who know what it's like.

Thank you to the ghosts of places and people
who make our lives what they have been.

Printed in Great Britain
by Amazon

31973296R00101